MARK RAMSDEN
wide variety of professio
related, although also wi
luminaries, including Tom
Baby'). He has also been a _____ psychic
and astrologer and the editor of cutting-edge sex
magazine *Fetish Times*. His serious music occasionally
surfaces on Radio 3 and his pierced and weighted
genitalia appear far too often in magazines and on
television. A sober alcoholic with a taste for hallucino-
genics, he lives in London with his partner, their son
and a discarnate entity called Lola.

His first novel, *The Dark Magus and the Sacred Whore* was also published by Serpent's Tail.

Also by Mark Ramsden and published by Serpent's Tail

The Dark Magus and the Sacred Whore

'A dryly witty murder mystery . . . the writing quality is superior, the style fast-paced and darkly comic . . . this is definitely one for those who believe SM fiction shouldn't be reduced to the level of Mills & Boons with bondage' *Skin Two*

'A baroque, uproarious parody of every genre you could think of . . . you'll laugh along until your piercings ache' *Time Out*

'A neo-noir tale of perversion and madness, and a wildly offbeat love story. Well worth a look! *Preview*

'A weirdly entertaining romp involving bodies in freezers, foot fetish videos, the roadie from hell . . . It's exactly the sort of book for which maverick publishing houses like Serpent's Tail were designed' *Forum*

'Cheese graters, rubber, ageing rock stars, black magic internet sites, dead drug dealers, missing penises, dodgy Sarf London geezers, cocaine and cyberincest in New York. Perverted, witty and absolutely hilarious debut' *Stuff*

The
DUNGEONMASTER'S APPRENTICE

Mark Ramsden

Library of Congress Catalog Card Number: 99–63333

A catalogue record for this book is available from
the British Library on request

First published by Serpent's Tail,
4 Blackstock Mews, London N4 2BT

Website: www.serpentstail.com

Phototypeset in Caslon by Intype London Ltd
Printed in Great Britain by Mackays of Chatham, plc

10 9 8 7 6 5 4 3 2 1

For the author of *Penetrating Wagner's Ring* (which really does exist, I'm not making it up) Thanks for the laugh, mate.

And for Dagmar – You're the one.

1

'GOLDEN JADE STROKED the pale moon of Sarah's bottom, the tips of her blood-red fingernails gently scratching the downy surface of her jutting curves.' I am reading from my own twisted scrawl, and if this is thought to be inappropriately salacious I should point out that there is a cash prize for the best piece of erotic writing at this party. In any case it's difficult to concentrate while my partner Sasha is having her bum tattooed, right here, right in front of me. She is lying face down while a young Eurasian woman swabs the curves of her right buttock with a piece of cotton wool soaked in something sharp and astringent. Sasha's shiny red rubber skirt has been draped over a nearby chair next to her 'Kill 'em all, let God sort 'em out' baseball cap. She is wearing fishnet stockings, silver DMs and a Torture Garden T-shirt, the one with the blood spattered over a crouching rubber-wrapped woman. Sasha's black rubber pants are rolled down to what some call the sulcus and the rest of us would say was the top of the thighs.

'Maybe it should be "twin moons", not "pale moon",' I say.

'That sucks,' says Sasha, the second I draw breath. Before I can tell her to do better, she is off. She only has to close her eyes and the muse kicks in full throttle. Which is not annoying, not at all.

'Only in the moment of surrender to Mary Lou Kim was Alice truly free,' she says, in a voice bearing no trace of her native Michigan. 'As Mary pushed her gently past the limits of her submissive desires, her body sang with pleasure as the whip cracked down on her again and again.'

Sasha flashes me a quick triumphant pout that melds into a wince as the eight-needle tattoo gun gets to work again. I might as well tell you she is five foot two, as it's the song that's always playing in her head. Never mind the bewitching eyes, the gap-toothed smile, her teased and twisted short blonde hair and the perfect skin tone; she is too small so she might as well kill herself.

That particular decision might well be out of her hands, for this very afternoon we received a package containing the skull of a dead cat, our names written backwards in something that may be blood, a picture of the two of us that had been torn to shreds and the neatly typed words, 'You will not escape the Dungeonmaster's Apprentice'.

Although this threat sounds like the invitation to a theme pub or a tourist trap, it was quite disturbing because, until tonight, no one was supposed to know we are even in London never mind our exact address. However, we shouldn't dwell on what might happen. 'Sufficient to the day the evil thereof,' as a minor Galilean cultist used to say. I'm more concerned about Sasha beating me to the Porno Olympics writing prize. I had been hoping to get in some helpful criticism of her effort, but so far she has left me with nothing to complain about.

'Each time the whip landed it left a white line which soon

blossomed into an angry red welt. As her flesh burned she croaked out a request for more. And more. Harder! Harder!'

Sasha's voice spirals down into some soft dream zone until she opens one eye to check the effect she is having on her audience. Not me, of course; she already knows I'm hooked. She is eager to see how this is going down with the Eurasian woman.

'More! More!' says the tattooist. 'Don't stop now! Whip her good!'

They share a smile of recognition. I don't have to worry about not smiling, because no one's looking at me.

'Your turn,' says Sasha slowly. She is breathing deeply to try to ride the wave of pain that isn't going to quit till her red rose tattoo is history. A brief smile establishes that the tattooist isn't going to join in, also that she is cute enough to quell any anxiety about the coming ordeal. Until I met her I hadn't been looking forward to getting my tattoos covered up, but since seeing her smile I have made plans for a full body suit of whatever design she wishes.

'There's too much of it now anyway,' says Sasha. 'I'm sick of the commodification of eroticism.'

I hate that kind of talk, which could be why she said it. If it's actually true it is bad news, for it means we will be earning a living from my visiting tarot service and the royalties from my compositions. The last one of these was broadcast at 3.43 a.m. on Radio 3 to an audience that may have been smaller than the small string ensemble involved.

'Does that mean I have to sell my body now?' I say. 'Better cancel that trip to Acapulco. It's Blackpool this year.'

'Oh, I don't know,' purrs Sasha, one dimple appearing as she gives me a skewed smile. 'Grant Mitchell lookalikes are big at the moment.'

I put my fists inside my shiny PVC jacket so she can't see I've clenched them.

'You know I hate *EastEnders* even more than that pretentious crap. "Commodification", my arse.' I tried not to sound annoyed, but she knows the difference.

'If you grew your hair you'd look like Grant Mitchell.'

'And if you stopped dying your hair blonde you'd look like Betty Boop.'

'Who?' says the tattooist.

'A cartoon babe with big, big eyes and a squeaky voice,' I explain.

'I don't have a squeaky voice,' says Sasha.

All of a sudden this is very important, and I know what to say the next time she annoys me. Which shouldn't be long because we are in our sixth year of cohabitation. We are more in love than ever, but six years is a long time to spend in that strange three-legged race of being a couple, hobbling off more or less in the same direction, each one hampering the other. No, as we are both potential witnesses for the prosecution of the other, we can't split up anyway. Can we? No, we can't. And just keep telling yourself that, my boy.

'You would definitely win the Porno Olympics,' I tell Sasha. 'Even writers are supposed to be good-looking now, and who could ever compete with you?'

She doesn't respond, but somewhere deep down she must have liked that. I try not to think that the tattooist could actually give her a run for her money while Sasha says some nonsense about words being more important than appearances. She doesn't believe it, of course; it's just because I have just said the opposite.

Spoken-word gigs always highlight the considerable contrast between the dream and grim reality. Let's face it. Real writers are often embarrassing in the flesh. Most of them have faces like arses without the crack in the middle. I doubt if the people about to read will be any different. Usually when the words are good, the performances don't work, and when the people are cute, the words don't work.

'That's nice, Cathy,' says Sasha in response to the drill. 'It's like being scratched by your favourite cat.'

Is it indeed? At least I can now remember Cathy's name. I have been told once already, but a quarter-century of incautious ingestion of bad chemicals has left me without a memory, cast adrift in a permanently confusing present. That's my excuse anyway. Sasha says this short-term memory stuff is just a media virus and will be forgotten in a few years' time. Well, it certainly will be by me. Cathy, Cathy, Cathy. I'm going to hold on to it this time.

'At least I don't look like a Millwall supporter with a day job,' says Sasha, still snapping at my heels.

'Thank you, but even a bloody colonial like you should know that the worst hooligans actually do have day jobs. It's an expensive business.'

Sasha turns her head away from me with the familiar pout that signals I am not worth arguing with.

'How are you coping?' asks Cathy, pausing in her drilling. Once she wipes the blood away from Sasha's punctured buttock, the red rose tattoo is still visible under the outline of the ram of Aries which will take its place.

'I've done this before, honey,' says Sasha, flashing Cathy a big beaming smile that seems a little over the top to me. Sasha shifts her hips, and there is a small, barely audible jangle of intimate body jewellery. It's a sweet sound but also reminds me that these piercings have all been photographed and published in every known format.

Sasha used to be a highly visible member of the Lower East

Side artistic community. Supreme Ogress Sasha, the only dim-inutive platinum blonde Art/Fetish/Occult Goddess with a worldwide fanbase. She was a little bit famous anyway, what with her dead rock-star husband and occasional court appearances whenever the police wished to question the validity of colonic irrigation as a fit subject for performance art. Now we are fugitives we are having to cover up our old tattoos, an arduous, painful and heartbreaking process as these were beautiful pieces of custom work. We put it off for as long as possible, but a private party in a body-art studio seemed to be a good place to get started. Even we couldn't disagree about this.

I don't really feel like a John Shaw and Sasha sure as hell doesn't want to be June Leah, but these were the only dead people our age we could find on a moonlit walk through Streatham Cemetery. John Shaw sounds dull but timeless, like my real name, Matthew Jackson, but June Leah sounds like a 1950s Jewish starlet even though she was born, like Sasha, in the late 1960s.

'Where's Tanya?' I say, naming the studio's resident piercer.

Cathy smiles, revealing deep dimples, almost the match of Sasha's own.

'They got rid of her. She was a lesbian and she was piercing the men slower. So it would hurt.'

'She was all right to me,' I say, rather surprised by this rev-elation.

'Yes, you're *so* good with women,' says Sasha, and all of a sudden it's gone dark in here. We could do with putting the heat on too. It's that tone of voice she often uses when she becomes Supreme Ogress Sasha for the punters and, as I keep telling her, it's supposed to be kept for their benefit only.

'It's a couple thing,' I say to Cathy, but she is concentrating very hard on carving out her patterns into Sasha's flesh.

'Alice sighed softly as Golden Jade covered her haunches with oil scented with sandalwood,' says Sasha, perhaps inspired by Cathy stanching the flow of blood with a tissue.

'I never liked "haunches",' I say.

'You could have fooled me,' says Sasha, giving her hips another wiggle and smiling broadly.

In another time and space this would be wonderfully invigorating, like a swig of Rémy Martin straight from the bottle to greet a new day. But the gentle undulation of her finest feature may well have been for Cathy's benefit and, yes, I am jealous. Thanks for sharing that.

'It's hardly erotic, is it? Haunches?' I say. 'You might as well say flanks . . . or split cushion of flesh, twin hams . . .'

'I hate hams,' says Sasha, who would leave me instantly if she ever saw me guiltily eating my bacon sandwich in the local café. 'Pale moon is better.'

'Yes,' I say. 'We have the dark mystery of the eternal female, the ever-changing moon . . .'

'Shut him up before he gets to Jungian archetypes,' says Sasha, propping her face up on two steepled hands so she can beam a fond smile back at me.

I get a jolt from that one, doubly so for it is a relief to feel the old ache again. Sometimes there is only a pale flicker of the old response, and you start to worry about the next few decades chained together with no time off for good behaviour. Some forms of bondage are anything but thrilling.

'So it's poetic,' I say. 'Sue me.'

'Someone should. What's wrong with "the cheeks of her ass"?'

I start to wave my hands around to facilitate thought, an American habit I picked up from Sasha.

'It's too bald, no resonance, it doesn't say anything.'

'I've never been in a situation where you wanted asses to say anything,' says Sasha.

The tattooist laughs, a deeper, coarser sound than I had expected from looking at her face.

'It's a peach,' she says, staring at the canvas she is presently working on.

'You're not wrong,' I say, but Sasha's nod of thanks is perfunctory. She can't even be bothered with flattery from her old man while Cathy is around. If I didn't know any better I'd say she was already falling in love. But it's probably infatuation and will hopefully be short-lived, like her recent passions for feng shui, tap-dancing and auric massage.

As today is Friday – sacred to Venus – I could drown this particular kitten by lighting a pink candle and some jasmine incense which, as we all know, would strengthen our relationship. It never fails. Apparently.

But the way Sasha is looking I'm going to need a crucified toad, a photo of Cathy, some pins to stick in it and a moonlit word with My Lord Lucifer. Perhaps I'm being over-sensitive – it wouldn't be the first time – but Sasha will get a crick in her neck if she carries on flirting like this.

The smile she is beaming at Cathy is an extra-large cappuccino effort, a real heart-starter with the extra sugar of the endearing gap in her front teeth, the dimpled cheeks and those big pupils filling up her big round eyes that may be turquoise or ultramarine or jade or . . . I won't be coming to a decision right now because my partner will be looking at Cathy for the foreseeable future. Sasha is doing everything except rolling over on her back, paws in the air, and asking for her belly to be tickled.

The object of all this adulation is presently clenching her lips while she concentrates on cutting along the line of the earlier markings. Sasha closes her eyes and moans as the tattoo gun gets to work again. The air is heavy with the scent of skunk from the party next door, rubber gear, some jasmine oil that Sasha is wearing and something that is probably only in my imagination: the scent of blood and singed flesh.

'Write this down,' Sasha sighs, as the little motorised razor gun in Cathy's hand starts to cover up the red rose, which has adorned the lower curves of her left buttock for as long as I've known her.

'Alice surrendered herself to the clean cut of the crop, pushing out her jutting ass cheeks to encourage Golden Jade to brand her with her special crest, a coiled riding crop.' There is a brief hush while the miniature razors of the tattoo gun cut into the skin. Sasha and I both know from bitter experience that brands usually spread into an ugly indistinct blob, but there is no doubt that she has come up with an arresting sentence. It's certainly got my attention, for it seems an open invitation to Cathy. It seems to be saying, 'As soon as we can shake granddad off, we can have some *real* fun'.

'You have a nice touch,' says Sasha sleepily. She must be getting just the right flood of endorphins from the needle gun, or maybe it's the insistent thudding bass drum from the party outside which is lulling her into a trance. Her eyes are closed tight as she hums something indeterminate.

'Casting any curses, honey?' I say. The buzzing of the razors continues.

'You're still here, aren't you?' she says. 'No, the moon is in Libra. It's just too conciliatory.'

'Hmm,' I say, being the safest thing I could think of. I would in any case rather concentrate on the rear view of Sasha's beautiful body and its presently most prominent feature. I strike out pale moon and try 'twin mounds' and then 'pert flesh' before briefly settling on 'chubby cheeks' before realising it is patronising and,

anyway, Sasha would kill me because 'chubby' has vague conno-
tations of surplus flesh. It's hard to concentrate what with the
thump and clatter of drum 'n' bass all around and the shrieks
and whoops of the dancers. I already know that if I ask Sasha if
she wants a drink she will say 'Yes!' too quickly and too enthusi-
astically, but it still hurts all the same.

'What would you like to drink, Cathy?' I say.

'No alcohol. No sugar. No caffeine. No dyes or e-numbers.'

From the way she is barking out her instructions it's as if I
had suggested cracking open a bottle of Slivovitz before going
on to drink Special Brew with the alkies underneath Waterloo
Bridge.

She looks up from her work and sees my slightly startled
expression. 'Sorry. I can't drink alcohol.'

'Just like old misery guts over there,' adds Sasha helpfully.

'And I try to keep fit,' says Cathy.

'Water or fruit juice, then?'

She nods approval and fires up her motorised scalpel once
more.

I put away my shiny black policeman's notebook, with its thick
restraining elastic band, and wander off into the swirling vortex
of the dance floor. It takes ten minutes to find supplies of warm
orange juice and cracked plastic glasses, and on my return I am
stopped in my tracks by the sight of Sasha and Cathy through
the door I left ajar. They can't hear my footsteps because of the
music which is so loud that I am craving the sanctuary of
the tattoo parlour, but something is going on that I can't intrude
on. Sasha lies there with her eyes closed. She looks to be sleeping
blissfully, perhaps dreaming of something pleasant. Cathy is
staring intently at the tattoo she is creating. It was no surprise
that she would want to scrutinise her work minutely; tattooists
usually take on a demonic air of concentration as they get into

their work. What I hadn't expected was for her to dip a finger in the wound she has opened on Sasha's flesh and for her to lick the blood slowly and reverentially, her eyes closing as the metallic taste hits her tongue.

2

Watching Cathy, my latest obsession, tasting the blood of Sasha, my one and only, roots me to the spot for the moment. There is a slight smile on Sasha's face, but she can't know what Cathy is doing. Unless she has slipped out for one of her quick astral strolls, in which case she will be having a laugh at my expense as I stand here listening to the blood rushing through my ears. Cathy's eyes are still closed as she slowly removes her fingers from her mouth, her glistening purple nails now licked clean.

I shouldn't really be thinking about any stubborn sticky bits in the quicks of her nails and whether I might be allowed to lick those clean. Or . . . no, never mind about that. It's probably time to do something useful like carry on breathing but, even if her little hobby is just a harmless kink, it's unsettling. I'm hardly in a position to throw stones, considering the state of the glasshouse I live in, but I'm not sure whether we want to surrender our flesh to a bloodsucking tattooist.

Once my conscious mind has done the parental guidance stuff warning me to beware strange women with quite possibly life-threatening diseases, I can relax and picture Cathy getting to work on my chest with a sharp implement, carving out a lurid tattoo while simultaneously draining my tethered body of every drop of sweat, blood and sperm. Which is all very well, but I'm still stuck in the corridor, afraid to move in case it breaks her trance. Her eyes are still closed as she savours the taste of Sasha's latest vintage. I shouldn't stand and stare, but it's infinitely preferable to going back in there and pretending not to be infatuated while I knock things over and talk too much.

Cathy's eyes open and she sees me. She looks flustered, as well she might. I shake my head and shrug to indicate she doesn't have to tell me about it, whatever it is. Then she gives me a freckle-bedecked smile and any further resistance is futile.

Now my trainee lapdog status has been settled it's best to run away before Sasha can find out. I deposit the drinks on the table, mumble something even I don't understand, and exit, after sharing one more conspiratorial smile with Cathy. The warm glow from that look protects me from the squelching synths, stomach-gouging kick drum and sampled screaming on the sound system as I wander through the mob trying not to think about my aching feet. The quietest room available contains a copulating couple and a nude man covered in clothes pegs undergoing a very slow caning from a witch with hennaed hair. There may not be freshly ground coffee available or a comfortable armchair and a selection of newspapers, but in the circumstances this is the best possible place for a nice sit-down. I sink gratefully to the floor and close my eyes. The first image to superimpose itself on the darkness is Cathy's smile. This will certainly crop up during my next Tantric self-massage session, although therapeutic prestidigitation is not likely to be high on the agenda until we know who is sending us death threats. Actually, knowing all that stuff is not likely to bring peace of mind either, for we would still have to do something about it. Or run away again, which seems more likely.

Sasha didn't seem particularly impressed by our surprise gift of blood, bones, fur and a recent photo of ourselves, but I find black magic death threats harder to ignore. Even sat here trying not to look like a voyeur while watching two people shag each other from close range, I'm still concentrating on the photo. It was taken recently outside the sort of non-aspirational working man's café that offers charred sausages, slippery fried eggs and twice-fried chips. Whoever took it must also have followed us back to our third-floor terraced council flat just south of the Elephant and Castle, or maybe they know the address from being one of Sasha's clients. She's a therapist, you know. Awfully good at relieving tension. I help count the money, in case you were wondering.

I unfold the note and study it, which gets me nowhere until I remember a collage Sasha once put together of her lifestyle submissives' handwritten letters, an utterly tragic collection of pitiful, bleating, whining . . . hang on, they've got me at it now.

Sasha's slaves are drawn from a wide variety of different backgrounds but their handwriting is uncannily similar. There must be a college somewhere – or perhaps a mail-order training programme – for they all had very small crabbed writing, often just capital letters strung together. The words 'you' and 'she' were usually in capitals and 'i' was often in lower case. The cataclysmically terrible spelling was surprising, given that they had all been soundly thrashed often enough to satisfy the most rigorous of Victorian pedagogues. They did, of course, have a vested interest in making mistakes. That our note is typed neatly does not necessarily rule out a submissive man, for several of her slaves are switches who like both extremes of the pendulum. As many of these men can be vicious sadists on their own turf, it is far from impossible that our package came from their ranks.

The word 'dungeonmaster' would certainly suggest that our stalker is a lifestyle perve, 'dungeonmaster' being scene jargon for the man who makes sure that the games players don't go too far and that orgy etiquette is respected. Apart from the obvious inference that the Dungeonmaster's Apprentice is a scene player – probably big and beefy enough to take over eventually from a dungeonmaster, someday, somewhere, somehow – and that this person owns a camera, I am no further than I was earlier on. I may be in love with Cathy also, but it's best not to dwell on that sort of thing. It should go away in a few days or so with any luck.

Sasha seemed to take the arrival of the package remarkably well, insisting that my fears are just another manifestation of black coffee psychosis. Perhaps I should have shown her the cat's head, but on balance I was right not to. One look at the dark red, fibrous material jutting out from the neck, or the nail driven through its forehead, and we would have had to use our antique straitjacket for its original purpose – the subjugation of the hopelessly insane.

She also ventured the opinion that perhaps my own activities as a bogus psychic and freelance curse-lifter and exorcist might have provoked this threat and, while it's true that some punters get the hump after paying hundreds of pounds for various magical services that they feel may not have significantly altered their lives, I thought I had covered that by advertising as a Karmic Astrologer and Tarot Consultant. I always explained carefully that the fruits of my labour may not truly manifest until the next life but one. Some people are in such a hurry. Actually, the sort of people who would hire a magus from a classified ad should be too frightened to try to take revenge, at least if I'm doing my job properly, but you never know. *I* never know anyway. The only thing I can forecast accurately is that Sasha will generally pull whoever I have been smitten with, and that by the time she has chewed them up and spat out the bones I never feel hungry any more.

Which is all very well, but sitting here listening to the porcine grunting of the couple making love and the slow irregular thwack of cane on buttock is not a fit occupation for a forty-one-year-old man. Neither is searching for party chemicals probably, but I want some so I am forced to go and mingle once more, an experience that does nothing to disabuse me of the notion that the finest companions for an evening's entertainment are a comfortable couch, a handful of psilocybin mushrooms and a widescreen television. There are far too many people crammed into this small space, a tattooing and piercing parlour tucked in behind Waterloo Station. We are within walking distance of Central London, but this part of Lambeth seems strangely resistant to gentrification. The street where Tribal Tattoos is situated is usually full of market stalls and the cheery banter of cockney costermongers. ('What's that? I can't hear you, you cant!' 'Well, I can't fackin' hear *you*.' Measured pause. 'Cant!')

I watch the mob getting drunk and aggressive from inside my isolated bubble of uptight sobriety. There are piles of discarded blue cans underfoot. I never understood why the very strong beer brewed in Germany tastes like beer or barley wine, and the stuff that British breweries make for the homeless tastes like liquid rust, but someone keeps buying it. I must be wrong, as usual. Clouds of hydroponically assisted London homegrown waft through the hall, propelled by the coughing and retching of those smoking it. This stuff engenders genuine hallucinations when smoked pure and will also wipe out any troublesome memories or excess brain cells. You won't have to join the French Foreign Legion to forget that disastrous love affair; a few lungfuls of this stuff and you can kiss your past goodbye – and your lungs, for that matter. Plus you will save on soap and water and work clothes because you will probably decide not to bother doing anything other than filling up the fridge and emptying it. Still hungry, you will probably end up scavenging through the bin to see if there's anything edible left in there. Better stock up on doughnuts now if you are going to get serious about it.

Gurning dancers would seem to indicate that someone has found some real Ecstasy while the beaming wrecks struggling to stand up could be ketamine casualties. Or perhaps it's just the booze which is giving them that out-of-body experience. There are also small clusters of people around mirrors dotted with white powder. The owners of these substances are basking in the warmth of the servile smiles their courtiers are directing at them. As I sip my warm, flat mineral water I remind myself that you don't need drink or drugs to enjoy yourself. Oh, no.

I know Sasha's looking for some toot, 'just to get Cathy's knickers off', but I'm not entirely sure I should encourage that. I could go home, I suppose, but the thought of waiting for Sasha to arrive arm in arm with Cathy and then having to listen to them fuck would be too humiliating for words. I carry on opening doors in a futile search for silence and a large comfy armchair, eventually finding the room where the Porno Olympics will be held.

The writing competition was supposed to be fun, but already people are bitching about the rules, the prize, the sponsors, *especially* the sponsors, a magazine which has had the cheek to provide free drink and food and run a successful business, unlike the people doing the complaining. There is a cluster of people around a tall guy with long silver hair and glittering eyes. He spots me and laughs out loud. Perhaps he is remembering that he once threatened to kill me, perhaps he is thinking about what a wizard wheeze it would be to send me another skinned cat. I wonder what Richard Ambrose is up to these days.

3

'PORNO EXCLUDES PEOPLE, especially women. *I* write erotica,' Richard is saying. I walk faster so I won't be able to hear any more, but the damage is already done. I'm starting to seethe, one of my major talents. For once I'm not alone.

You don't have to know Richard to dislike him intensely, but once you do the habit is very hard to kick. Right now he is playing with one of his magical toys, a custom-made dagger that has been blessed, or more likely cursed, by an occult blacksmith. The hilt of the weapon is set with glittering stones, and there are occult squiggles inscribed on the blade, combinations of basic runes called bindrunes. Many of those standing around trying to look unimpressed would dearly love to drive this implement into his back if they could, but they all need something from him. He is, of course, not unaware of their real feelings towards him but puts the constant sniping behind his back down to jealousy. Unfortunately there is a lot to be jealous of. As he will remind you if you let him. Incidentally, some literary authorities apparently feel that useful information about people's characters and motivations should only be gleaned from what they say and not from these miniature biographies. While this may be so, they probably haven't been to many dance venues recently. Thanks to the invigorating blast of drum 'n' bass I can't hear what Richard is saying, and I doubt if the person standing right next to him can either. You will just have to put up with my admittedly biased version of his character until they turn that stuff off.

Richard has inherited wealth, poise and prominent cheekbones that he keeps honed by taking large quantities of real uncut cocaine and smoking heavily. He is about six and a half superfluous feet tall. I can't really see up that far, but suffice to say that his head is in a different time zone to most of Sasha and, as with the Canary Wharf Tower, even people who hate the sight of him have to admit to a certain grudging respect. His silver hair is still luxuriant enough to be worn long, although the bastard must be fifty. He is wearing something that looks like an SS uniform, although the silver badges and buttons are subtly different from the original. It's still enough to jangle the nerves and set alarm bells ringing. You can almost hear the hackles rising as he struts through the club.

What is worse, he has not squandered his inheritance and uses only enough drugs to enjoy himself. He likes fast cars but won't drive recklessly enough to kill himself. He is reckless but has no interest in self-destruction. He is supposedly good at some esoteric branch of the martial arts, and even if he isn't he could just fall on you from that height. I need a drink just thinking about him, but I can't have one, ever again, so I'm just going to have to go on being annoyed. Which is even easier than usual, for Richard has brought his big frightening dog with him, a Rhodesian Ridgeback called Stanley. Someone shuts the door and we can all hear Richard's genuine patrician voice once more and the cockney accent that comes and goes.

'Erotica can never be packaged or marketed,' Richard is saying to a heavy-set scowling man who doesn't want to hear it. 'What you do is show business, my dear.'

'You need technical skills to do what we do,' says the same broken-toothed beer drinker. His cheap leather jacket is scuffed, his black jeans are dangerously close to casual leisurewear, a contemptible mode of dress worn by wage slaves and people who still live with their mums. The beer drinker's belly is going in and out faster now as he draws inspiration from a couple of quick swigs of Becks.

'Real plots, rounded characters, believable dialogue.' More beer. 'All the things you're too *brilliant* to bother with.'

Well, he can glower all he likes; Richard is still rich. He kisses his blustering adversary full on the lips, after which the guy can only empty his bottle then scurry off for more. Sasha told me earlier that she was looking to meet some group of erotic writers with a view to tidying up some of her sex novels for mainstream publication. I doubt that she would feel much in common with this haggard old hack or that she would want to remove all references to drugs and contemporary reality just to get a few grand. These harassed-looking professionals usually churn out cheap paperbacks that sell only because they have covers featuring the sort of 'glamour' models who wear their names around their necks in gold. They don't do much for me, these women with permed hair and blank, stupid faces. They look less like an invocation of Lilith the Dark Goddess than what they actually are: Essex girls who are saving up for a hairdressing salon.

Richard's writing is, of course, on a higher plane to the rest of us even though he managed only a few books of poetry before retiring from the world of literature to mire himself in the darkest, most forbidden areas of the occult – as if writing poems with Latin titles wasn't obscure enough already. His latest offering is bound in speckled calf and ocelot. The title is blocked in gold leaf, there are marbled endpapers and it's printed on paper made from virgin aardvarks' tongues. This lavishly illustrated treatise on where the mage Paracelsus went wrong costs around five hundred pounds. There's a few left. Finally, there are the private journals he writes in blood, ink and semen for the purpose of various sex magick operations. It's best not to get mentioned in one of these tomes if you can help it. If you hadn't already guessed, his father practically runs one of the high-street banks. That's what's paying for all this.

While I'm obsessing over Richard a slide of Sasha in her former incarnation flashes up on the wall. She looks quite magnificent, but it is also a reminder that going undercover isn't really an option for exhibitionists. It is hardly a surprise that the Dungeonmaster's Apprentice has managed to track us down.

Richard grabs the mike then bangs a gong to attract everyone's attention. By the time he has banged it about ten more times he has just about managed to get people to look at the stage. Once it gets through to the drunker guests that they will have to stop screeching at each other for a while, there is a general rush for the door. Soon no one is left except people feverishly reading and rereading their competition entries.

Richard is bouncing around in his jackboots grinning at everyone and getting a servile response back. Whenever he alights on the likes of me, who churlishly refuse to play along, he just cranks up the smile a notch or two. It's very effective and very annoying.

'Matt! It is Matt, isn't it? Why aren't you dancing?' he says. 'Look at you! Too scared to enjoy yourself. Live a little!'

'You're fifty, aren't you?' I say. He guffaws and claps me on the back, which is every bit as annoying as you might imagine it to be.

'I'm fitter than the average twenty-year-old,' he says. 'I love to dance. I always have, I always will. Whereas you are locked into some eighteenth-century ideal of the importance of the individual. The only thing that matters is the collective, dear. The dance.'

'I suppose if you have just made a couple of grand knocking out Es to these . . . sheep, it must look absolutely wonderful.'

It's not a secret that Richard often provides the fuel for these parties, so I just sound jealous and bitter, as I often do. The dismissive hand flourish I aim at the dance floor looks nothing like I thought it would and looks even worse when Richard imitates it, not once but many times, eventually incorporating it into a little dance sequence, which at least has the benefit of taking him away from me.

Some time later, when my pulse has returned to normal, Sasha and Cathy arrive, sharing the sort of smile that makes me wonder what else they have been sharing recently. I can't wait to see Sasha's new tattoo, but it will be well wrapped up for the moment so that she doesn't bleed all over her rubber skirt. They wander over to where I am just as Richard mounts the podium to introduce someone wearing a pirate costume, whose head is obscured by a huge inflated rubber mask.

4

THE RUBBER PIRATE cringes and mopes around the stage for a while trying not to occupy the space he is standing in, although another part of him is strangely insistent, like a cat that is not going to go away until it has got some smoked salmon – none of that Whiskas rubbish for me, thank you very much.

Sasha whispers up towards my ear, 'Hugh Dick.'

I didn't recognise our most lucrative client in his party cozzy, but the only thing that matters now is trying out an oldie-but-a-goodie on Sasha.

'*You're* a dick,' I say.

'No! Hugh Dick!' she says and then notices the satanic gleam in my eye. I have actually won at something for the first time in weeks. 'Oh, grow up,' she says, a rare admission of defeat. Hugh is still stumbling around the stage, just about falling off as he tries to position himself to read his entry. He has always been a bit touchy about his name, although he has never gone so far as to insist it's really pronounced 'dee-ack'.

Good old Hugh. We are already several thousand pounds richer due to Sasha's regular visits to his Docklands flat. Just don't tell anyone that she often nips out for a quick J and a line while Hugh is safely tucked up in his rubber romper suit, fervently worshipping the divine one. As we know from the tireless efforts of the apologists for consensual torture, everyone involved in s/m is an entirely responsible pillar of society who puts the welfare of their slaves first and foremost, never drinks or abuses drugs and never does anything to their slaves that they do not want to be done. I myself am the reincarnation of Napoleon Bonaparte and Sasha has just perfected a cure for cancer which she will market when the time is right.

'Look at that guy!' says Sasha, as another fat submissive approaches on all fours. I cast a jaded eye in his direction but end up nodding approval for some serious tattoos. All the way across his back is the word 'Service' in large Gothic script. Across his enormous shaven stomach is a large multicoloured tattoo of a weeping clown which would have been a very painful process. It's certainly painful to look at, being bright enough to warm your hands on. He has half a junkyard hanging off his nipples, and I dread to think what is stuck through his tackle, but there is no time for admiring body art any more; Hugh Dick has something of great importance he wishes to share with us. Not just yet, though. Now that everyone is looking at him, he has to start faffing about making feverish last-minute corrections to his text.

'I could do erotic fiction,' says Sasha, as the audience groans and hurls abuse at the stage.

'As you well know, commercial publishers won't touch anything to do with drugs, body art, which they would no doubt call self-mutilation, scat, non-consensual s/m . . .'

'So what?'

'So you couldn't "do erotic fiction" as you, rightly, like to please yourself.'

She is sulking now, although why she thinks being a literary whore will be better than being a real one I don't know. Her present clients literally kiss her arse, something which is unlikely to happen at the average literary lunch.

'Oh, sorry,' she says. 'Have I stepped on your turf? Maybe I should just take my clothes off and win the prize that way.'

'It has to be an evocation of the erotic muse in words.'

'Who makes up all these dumb ass rules? Has to be a man, right? They always try to control everything.'

'Which is why I always win in this relationship.'

'You always get your way.'

Which is news to me, but before we can get any further with that Hugh begins to talk about a fantasy slave ship where certain transgressions get such and such amounts of punishment, and how, and why, and . . . is that the time? More beer, anyone? . . . People start to shuffle about, and there is some mutinous whispering as his reading continues interminably. The unsuccessful attempt to ape a posh 1950s Home Counties voice doesn't help, or the feeble quavering light tenor he speaks in. It's almost as if he has been hired by some conservative think-tank to perpetuate the image of perves as sad old men who are incapable of normal congress. To add to the misery he is a Details Nazi, one of the many on the scene who become unbearably excited at long lists of forfeits and punishments. They demand to know if the tawse they are being thrashed with is from the recently discovered secret stash of John J. Dick, master tawse-maker from the small Fifeshire town of Lochgelly, or whether it is merely a cheap copy. Can one ever justify the use of non-PC terms of abuse during power-exchange games? Is permanent scarring permissible on a first date? Are uniforms and peaked caps acceptable or are they all too reminiscent of the SS?

This is something that Hugh doesn't have a problem with, those particular initials as he has them branded into his buttocks, where they signify Sasha's Slave. She sometimes asks me when I'm going to have mine done. I *think* she is joking.

Hugh suddenly removes the mask to reveal that his grey hair has gone lank and wayward, his pudgy face is red and sweaty and, unforgivably, he is sporting a full greying beard.

'Put the mask back on,' bellows some yob.

'Shut up!' Sasha hisses at me. 'Give him a chance.'

'I demand silence for my poem "In Honour of the Goddess",' he says. His voice trembles, and all of a sudden I feel on the brink of tears, real ones. Something about the battered and abused child Hugh obviously was gets to me for about one-fifth of a second and then normal service is resumed.

Hugh is still waiting for silence, but the blather continues relentlessly. His jowls and belly wobble as he stamps his foot. Well, if he thought he was going to silence a pack of drunks armed only with some poetry it's tough tits, it's just not going to happen. Just as he is about to walk off in a state of what I believe used to be called high dudgeon, Richard bellows, 'Silence!'

A drunk couple continue to monologue simultaneously, almost as loudly as if a double-bass player was playing a solo on stage. Richard goes over with his hound. 'Shut! The! Fuck! Up!' he says, very loudly and very slowly. The couple look indignant that someone dares to interrupt them, then they spot the slavering jaws of Stanley the Rhodesian Ridgeback and the runic sigil on his collar, which looks fascist to the uninitiated. The man tries to sneer, but something about Richard's face thrust right between the two of them kills it stone dead. The guy could easily punch Richard's jutting jaw and ironic placatory smile, but he is not up to it. Only the drunk or suicidal would be. Richard withdraws and bows towards the stage with a flourish that gets everyone looking at him again.

Hugh opens up once more with all the deadly oratorical force of John Major in full bleat. 'I would like to apologise to the assembled company, for although I know poetry has been disallowed, my relationship with the Dark Goddess is such that I will undergo any torture in order to sing her praises.'

He looks wistfully over at Sasha, which is inappropriate, as he knows.

'I'll skin him for this,' mutters Sasha.

'We could have him stuffed,' I whisper in her ear, which produces the queasy face I was hoping for. I notice that there is a purple smudge on her ear lobe. I look across to where Cathy is standing to check that it is indeed a similar purple to her lipstick. Perhaps Cathy has been whispering in her ear. Perhaps if Sasha were to undress right now I would find more of these purple smudges. Cathy might have been whispering in all sorts of places if I know Sasha.

'I once had to tattoo a poem on some guy's back,' says Cathy suddenly.

'Wow!' says Sasha. There might have been a time when she would have looked at me to share her delight. Tonight it is Cathy who gets the big, zonked eyes and the frazzling smile.

'The problem is you often grow out of these meaningful statements,' I say. 'Then you have to go back for an elaborate cover-up job.'

The way Sasha is looking at me you would think I had just suggested we bring back Hugh to have a scene at our place. Before she can get started on me a cough and a preliminary bleat announces that Hugh has summoned his muse.

No doubt he is about to prove why there is a ban on verse.

All I know about live poetry is that I seem to be functioning well enough without it, but you never know, maybe Hugh will change my mind.

'Dark Goddess, whose place has been so cruelly usurped by the nailed one,' intones Hugh.

'Fucking hell,' says Sasha, and she's not wrong. Heads turn towards us, but only to nod in approval. It was the stress on the second syllable of nailed which did it. Any more of this and Hugh is going to see for himself what it is like to be nailed to the stage, probably through something soft and sensitive. An ominous hubbub rises from the crowd as he continues.

'Wherever I am, I will serve you. I would lay down my very life. Offer you my heart, my soul, my breath, my eyes, my . . .'

There is more, but Hugh has made his point. He is sitting by the phone. His picture and CV have been circulated. He's available. If there is any doubt in the matter he takes out a small dagger and adds another knife slash to the ridged and mottled white flesh on his left forearm. Some amateurs gasp at this, but most people continue to stare with dead eyes. Party perves don't like to look shocked, not even with great gouts of claret dripping everywhere. Hugh closes his filofax but continues to drone on.

'As you may be aware, I have just committed an illegal act.'

'Commit another. Cut your fucking head off,' shouts someone, who may have been drinking. 'Are you sure you're a masochist? You're certainly hurting us, you sad old git,' the same rough London voice continues.

The performance somehow dribbles to a close and then, as Hugh probably intended, there is no applause and he is able to crawl off the stage and over to Sasha's feet. As he makes his way over the less than pristine stone floor he leaves a trail where the wet rubber soaks up the dust and fag ends left by the guests.

'He's like a slug,' says Richard, who has wandered over to us, grinning as always. 'We should spray him with salt and watch him dissolve.'

Which would be rather more entertaining than having him hovering around our kneecaps, gibbering and whimpering. Before Sasha can send Hugh packing, a disturbance breaks out in the mob, fairly obviously drink-related. Richard moves in with his yapping dog, which soon nips that one in the bud.

'Men!' says Sasha, shaking her head fondly.

I manage not to say anything unwise about Sasha's passion for pugilism, which is by no means confined to the noble art of boxing. She also likes bare-knuckle fights, arm wrestling, gut barging, headbutting and Thai kick-boxing, but most of all she likes fights on licensed premises – especially when she is the promoter and I am the Great White Hope to be matched against all-comers. Now we are sober there probably won't be any more bare-knuckle bouts that end in sudden death, but you never know with Sasha. She's a troublemaker.

'It's pathetic,' says Hugh, who seems to think he can stand up and talk with the grown-ups now. 'They're like two-year-olds deprived of the breast.'

This would carry a little more authority if I didn't know that Hugh possesses an impressive array of adult baby garments and has a fetish for fat, frumpy, lactating women. Which in any case is just a diversion from his real obsession, which is hanging; the theory and practice of judicial hanging, autoerotic strangulation, asphyxiation techniques – don't get him started on it, for you may find yourself roped in for one of his swinging parties. He's certainly versatile; just about the only thing he doesn't have a fetish for is sexual intercourse with young, attractive women. That's right out.

The problem is that Hugh, like many strangulation freaks, or the dangling wankers as the ambulance crews call them, tends to forget that these out-of-body experiences can become permanent. Well, I hope Sasha doesn't get engrossed in one of her battered old green Penguins while he is dancing the Tyburn Tarantella. Apart from the fact that his weight would probably put my back out, we can't afford, for legal reasons, to get involved in any more corpse disposal scenarios.

'Remove yourself, Hugh,' says Sasha.

'What have I done now?' I say.

She kicks me, near the ankle, where it hurts.

'Can you stop that pathetic gag now?' she says, as Hugh lumbers off to get on someone else's nerves. A twenty-something with a bumfluff goatee staggers past blankly before crashing into the drinks table. His resemblance to Kurt Cobain makes me want to get a few swift kicks in while he's down, but I have to keep that to myself as Sasha thinks he was Lord God Almighty. Still, if she didn't like these supposedly tragic losers I would be out of a job.

Two guys snuff up some amyl nitrate close by.

'I hate the smell of that stuff,' I say.

'Really?' says Richard, whom I wasn't addressing. 'I have no sense of smell. Rather convenient considering the people I have to deal with, don't you think?' He nods in the direction of the moiling mob and at Hugh who is presently waddling about, spreading his own brand of misery wherever he can find someone to stand still long enough. Richard tilts his chin upwards ever so slightly and holds the pose to remind us how damnably handsome he is before swanning off to torment someone else.

'Really?' I say, but I can't do Richard's voice. Or the poise or the charm or the cheekbones. Or the wealth. Well, let's not dwell on it. Too long.

As soon as Richard bounds on to the stage there is silence. This may be because he has immense charisma or it may be because he has whipped several of the assembled company to within an inch of their lives. Perhaps this is what is firing his intense dislike of me: I have yet to submit to his iron rod of discipline.

'Stalingrad Nights,' he announces, to sycophantic laughter. 'This legendary erotic diary of a gay soldier has somehow survived thanks to the perseverance of tank fetishist Ricard Silber, who runs a small press devoted to the underground network of gay Nazis who meet regularly on the anniversary of the Battle of Stalingrad to re-enact their earlier manoeuvres.'

He looks pointedly at Hugh as he continues, cranking up the sneer in his voice as he does so. 'As many of these old soldiers now need wheelchairs, walking sticks and Zimmer frames to move about at all, their attempts at rough sex now have a certain poignancy. If you are one of the growing fraternity that likes tanks, mud, crusted blood and German drinking songs mixed in with occasionally less-than-consensual geriatric gay sex, this could be for you. Also contains an exhaustive afterword by Huge Arse in which he uncovers the hitherto unknown strain of anti-Semitism in the Nazi Party.'

There are some appreciative howls and whoops from some of the shaven-headed men who are strutting about in jackboots and black peaked caps. One even has the twin sun runes of the SS on the lapels of his flawless Nazi uniform. I remember that Hugh considers himself to be a socialist and is obsessed with anti-Semitism while not being Jewish himself. Despite this, he accepts Richard's last remark with a weak smile. He's too busy fawning over Sasha anyway.

'Did my poem please you, mistress?' he says.

Sasha is now seated, one knee crossed over the other, and from the way her gleaming silver boots are tapping I would suspect a recent input of party chemicals. She chugs down some mineral water, for it is getting very hot indeed, then delivers a fearsome open-handed slap across his face. He gasps from the shock but is otherwise unharmed as I watch the red imprint of Sasha's gloved hand blossom across his wet chubby cheek.

'Will you accept my humblest . . .'

'Someone should plug up the airways into your head and let us watch you suffocate slowly,' says Sasha, and she's not acting now. As far as I will ever know. Hugh is whimpering. Although a fair amount of people are leering at Sasha – rightly so, in my view – there are those who are shocked by this sort of thing. The Fetish Police are here, those interfering busybodies who are trying to make this stuff respectable. As if repeating their 'Consensual Adult Roleplay' mantra endlessly on late-night talk shows will make any difference to thousands of years of Xtian bigotry. Be that as it may, it would be a brave dungeonmaster who felt up to the task of tapping Sasha on the shoulder and telling her to desist. In any case, she is far too busy cursing Hugh to notice anything else presently.

'The pleasure I got from watching you die would at least make up for having to look at your loathsome face,' she continues. 'Otherwise, your presence on the planet is a waste of natural resources. In fact, the only thing that could rescue this party is the sight of you flat on your back, all four limbs twitching spasmodically as you die a slow lingering death.'

Sasha does a spot of lingering herself over the last three words, then kicks him hard.

We have crossed over a line here. There is an etiquette, a strict etiquette you might say, that governs how mistresses and slaves behave. Genuine hatred isn't usually part of this. She stands there glowering at him while he stares resolutely at the floor beneath him. I remember that he is not even allowed to look at her boots unless she says so.

Her voice drops to a whisper, but she certainly doesn't need volume to make her point. 'I would like to take a dump right over your loathsome face as they lay you in your coffin.'

There are some twisted grins at this, but one woman in zebra make-up stomps out in disgust as Sasha's boots interface repeatedly with Hugh's flab. She then grabs the largest, blackest dildo I have ever seen and slips a rubber glove over her right hand. The dildo comes complete with realistic veins and a cute pink furry handle at the base. If the handle seems inappropriately girly, there is nothing effete about the look of grim determination on Sasha's face as she uses a small dagger to cut open his rubber playsuit around his anus and then starts to ram it right up his mulhadra chakra.

Even with lubrication, this would give you pause for thought, and he is soon emitting the sort of sounds that would bring tears to the eye of the most flint-hearted state torturer. It's just giving Sasha a taste for more, though. Someone should stop her really, but it's not going to be me. The Goddess Kali herself would be getting short shrift from my little Sasha in this mood. She looks like she is trying to plant the dildo inside him, somewhere up around his throat. Hugh is surprisingly vocal in his distress, something that hardly ever happens given his legendary appetite for punishment. Another fan of consensual s/m by numbers leaves at this point with the immortal words, 'You're sick.'

'Physician heal thyself,' I say. Sasha's head swivels quickly in my direction long enough to dispatch a thunderbolt which I take to mean, 'This is my space, go away and infest somewhere else.'

To save face, or to kid myself I'm saving face, I hang around for a while watching Hugh having the time of his life. If he had a tail it would be wagging now as Sasha plumbs his depths. I think she looks cute when she's working, all that concentration and that severe frown of hers, but as soon as Cathy aims her shiny boots towards the door my attention is immediately distracted.

As Sasha is practically up to her armpits in Hugh, I thought I could sidle out at this point without her noticing, but she tosses me a sneer as I pass her by. As I follow Cathy out, I remind myself that I have nothing in common with the slug men crawling around on the floor behind their mistresses. Then I remind myself several more times. And then I believe it. Almost.

5

No one bothers Cathy or tries to approach her as she weaves her way through the crowd. I remember Sasha's proud boast that, although a single woman might be harassed in a club for drunken normal people, your average perve would not dream of doing such a thing. It's true that fetish clubbers are often very concerned about politeness. You can usually expect an apology if anyone stands on your toe, which might seem odd, especially if that person is about to drip hot wax over someone's soft squidgy bits, but then such a complex game needs lots of rules.

Cathy stops by a merchandising stall, and the guy behind it with the waxed blond dreads falls for her instantly. She appears unmoved by his insistent patter and hopeful smile, rifling through the display before pointing out a T-shirt she likes.

'I'll just get these pins out,' he says, taking the shirt from the display.

'Leave them in,' says Cathy. 'I prefer it that way.'

He starts to laugh but then looks into her unsmiling face and sees something a lot colder and harder than he was bargaining for. I think of her penchant for plasma and wonder whether I will be able to persuade her to taste my blood at some point in the near future. The guy behind the counter now looks as if he would like to use the shirt to shine her thigh-length boots or, even better, just use his tongue to clean her all over while she inserts the pins at strategic points around his body. Actually, there might well be an element of what Freudian quacks call projection here, as this scenario has just taken my fancy. There are a few other party games that have also occurred to me, but we must get on.

Cathy buys a bottle of Evian then wanders through to a chill-out room full of beanbags and soft, tinkly music. This would be very relaxing if it weren't for a tall, very thin, very white woman with an enormous burn mark on her scrawny neck who is talking, and smoking, way too loudly. She is wrapped from head to toe in what might be real fur, and the subject of her monologue is her attempts to make her life as a dominatrix into a book. Or a movie. Or a musical. Or a documentary that will eventually be shot into space with other important cultural artefacts that will remain for ever available for any alien life forms who wish to be informed of the eternal evil that we call masculinity. To cut to the chase it would seem that so and so, whom I hadn't heard of, shouldn't be famous; men are bastards; men who are producers are complete bastards, and that life isn't fair. Her face is registering its usual distaste at the poor quality of her surroundings and the supporting cast she has been given to work with. She looks and sounds the same as she always did, although at some point her face has obviously fallen off and been stitched back on again, far too tightly, by a drunken seamstress.

I had hoped never to see Alice Hathaway-Turner again, but at least someone appears to have attempted to burn her to death in the interim, possibly herself, as she is still smoking long thin brown cigarettes through a pale jade holder which she waves through the air constantly. Yet another fat nude man is kneeling beside her, head on his chest, his hands cupped together to catch her cigarette ash. He either thinks that keeping a well-trimmed beard around the edges of his face minimises his sagging jowls or that it is aesthetically pleasing. He is wrong on both counts.

'I hope that's fake,' says Sasha, nodding vigorously in the direction of the fur wrap Alice is wearing. I didn't notice her creep up behind me, but then it's very loud in here.

I do hope Sasha is not going to have a go. Both potential protagonists have particularly sharp teeth and talons, and it's quite often the referee who gets the worst of it in these grudge matches. Sasha is now muttering ominously. Soon her head will start to rotate and she will projectile-vomit copious amounts of green bile all over Alice's coat. I had forgotten that in Sasha's alternative universe one dead mink is roughly the equivalent of the latest African famine.

'I never thought I'd ever see another fur hag,' says Sasha.

For some reason, probably because we live together, I have to put the other side of the argument. 'What about Sascher-Masoch? Without him you would be out of a job.'

For an instant Sasha looks like she's going to blitz me with a twenty-minute statement on Venus in Furs, speciesism and, most of all, why I should be ground up for catfood, but she is concentrating hard on Alice, who is talking about the presumption of some photographer who wanted her to pose for nude shots. In the middle of saying 'nasty little man' she coughs hard enough to loosen the linings of her lungs. Despite tears in her eyes and the undertow of rattling phlegm, she manages to gasp out her favourite phrase one more time while some other raddled old hag stands opposite, smoking in a grim and determined manner. Her schoolgirl outfit is a little optimistic under the circumstances.

'Who is she?' asks Sasha, staring very hard at Alice, who is still oblivious to us.

'It's Alice Hathaway-Turner,' I say. It's fun watching Sasha go through some of her repertoire of tics and tricks as this sinks in.

'Alice Hathaway-Turner?' There is some hand waving, eye swivelling and a double take that is way over the top but perhaps appropriate in this situation. 'That's what she's really called?'

'Certainly.'

'She looks like my grandma,' says Sasha.

'That's pushing it, surely,' I say. 'She can't be forty yet.'

'Some women become more beautiful with age,' says Sasha, and this comes free with her usual ironic quotation marks. Sasha has recently committed the heinous crime of hanging around the planet long enough to become thirty years old, but there is no way of telling her that she looks gorgeous. Well, there is, but she just won't hear it.

'Some dominatrixes start to believe the act eventually,' I say. 'She's got it bad.'

Amazingly enough, Sasha doesn't contradict this even though it's true and I said it.

'Is she famous?' she asks.

'Trying to be,' I say, thinking of a number of recent late-night television appearances.

'How do you know her?'

It's not really safe to tell her, but if I spend any longer trying to think of a version of events that puts me in a good light we will be here all night.

'It's a long time ago, but we used to go to the same dealer,' I say, 'who was her pimp before she got all high and mighty. I've actually seen Alice having a fistfight with some runaway from the provinces on her patch on Streatham Common. And before you ask, I was only there to buy dope.'

'Why would I care if you used sex workers?' says Sasha. 'You know I'm not jealous.'

'Hmm,' I say. It's too dangerous to say anything else.

'You know we have an open relationship.'

'Sounds like you're just reminding me you want to sleep with Cathy.'

'You can talk.'

'If you want to sleep with her, that's fine . . .'

'You bastard! Don't ever tell me what to do!'

'I didn't . . .'

'And don't patronise me!'

'I wasn't . . .'

'If you think I'm going to be some little wifey type sitting at home waiting for you to get home from your girlfriend, you can fuck right off!'

This quintessentially English expression sounds cute in Sasha's American accent so I make the mistake of smiling, or getting as close as I ever do to a smile without pscilocybin mushrooms. The sight of both sides of my mouth crinkling upwards for less than a second apparently merits the hurling of her half-full plastic mineral water bottle past my head. The projectile hits the wall behind me and lands safely, but the water ends up on some large guy in a studded leather jacket who accepts my shrug of apology.

Turning back to Sasha, who is still seething, it occurs to me to say that girls are crap at throwing things, but she doesn't seem to be in the mood for a joke. Not right now.

'There's no need to get mad,' I say, which has the opposite effect to the one intended. She starts shouting.

'Don't you dare say I'm mad. I am totally rational! At all times!'

Well, she doesn't look it right now, eyes ablaze and hands

twitching in all directions. There's times when I want this to happen and I can't say anything which will annoy her, and then there's this sort of inexplicable, and unwanted, victory.

'I'm sorry,' I say, holding out my own hands, palms upwards. There are no hidden weapons there but it's not quite enough just yet. She shakes her head and offers a weak smile to show that normal service is resumed. I think that's what she means. As we have only been living together for around six years now, it's too early to say. I breathe out slowly and decide to share something that has been bothering me ever since I spotted Alice.

'You know she was an occasional associate of Jason Skinner's,' I say.

Sasha picks up on the fear in my voice but shrugs. 'You worry too much.'

Jason was involved with us in a particularly trying set of ritual murders last Easter. He was a well-connected face, and it's sort of our fault he doesn't exist any more, although this may still be a secret. It is however definitely my fault that his brother is dead, and a lot of his relatives know this. As their sort of family takes a vengeful Old Testament view of murder, I tend to worry about them finding us. None of which seems to affect Sasha. 'There are still tabloid headlines about Jason even though no one knows where he is,' I say. 'You're telling me he won't have told any of his family or his dear old mum that he was looking for us?'

'Alice is hardly going to lead his family to us. No one knows who we are and where we live.'

Which isn't true, since we got that package.

'She could have sent the cat.' I'm wittering again, and Sasha isn't going to stand for it.

'Get over it! Any sex worker will get death threats all the time. Some of us end up dead. It's all part of the war men wage against women.'

I open my mouth to ask why she has somehow metamorphosed into a lesbian academic when a minuscule twitch at the corner of her mouth alerts me to the possibility that she is joking.

'Most amusing,' I say. 'Look, Jason must have mentioned he was looking for me to someone in his immediate family. They must be looking for his killer by now.'

'There is no body. No one can even prove he is dead. The only possible explanation is that one of my dad's old buddies from the CIA must have cleaned it all up. Who else would bother?'

Sasha is now lost in the body-art slides flashing up on the wall while I continue talking to myself about threatening letters, magickal attack by self-styled sorcerers, a possible imminent attempted murder by our stalker and the distinct possibility that running from New York to London has changed very little.

'Someone is out to get us,' I say, more than once, but I might as well be telling her about my last round of mini-golf for all the interest she is taking. You can usually rely on the murder of close friends and family to sustain a conversation, but Sasha has drifted off somewhere else – until the work of Annie Sprinkle comes up on the wall, when her whole face crumples then hardens into the sort of determined look that speaks of injustice and deadly revenge. The work is a picture of a raw egg, with the yoke intact, nestling in a woman's pubic hair, which appears similar to the sort of thing Sasha was doing as a deranged teenager but, as I have never had the courage to say to her face, Sasha wasn't exactly the first to perpetrate this stuff anyway.

Thankfully, she is still busy staring at Alice, probably trying to make her hair fall out with some spell or other. She definitely wants a scrap with someone, which makes me wonder whether Cathy has turned her down.

'I saw her hanging round Cathy earlier,' says Sasha.

'Well, you had better hurry up, then,' I say. 'Alice is famous for getting what she wants. And she doesn't like opposition.'

Alice finally realises that two people are staring at her and comes close enough for me to see that her neck is a lot scrawnier and scraggier than it was. My eyes flick back upwards to catch a megaton blast of loathing and contempt.

'Sorry,' I say. 'I couldn't help noticing.'

Her eyes are like tiny smouldering chips of black hash. Despite what I tell my clients I never could see auras, but I can actually feel this one: pure hatred, not cut with anything. You have to know someone special to get this stuff.

'Have you seen enough now? I was in a fire,' she says, like I set it. 'Even you must know it's vulgar to stare.'

There is a pause while she coughs, removes the stub of her pointlessly expensive cigarette from the holder and stubs it out on the fat man's back. Many on the scene would hardly notice such a fleabite, but this guy's skin is pristine: no scars, tattoos, brands, whip marks or welts. He either has a partner who doesn't know about his little hobby or he has just started. He squirms briefly then returns to his previous posture. The longer I spend here watching this, the stronger she feels, but I can't go without asking her if she is responsible for sending us our dead cat-o-gram.

'I don't suppose I should feel surprised that a shabby little pervert like you should turn up here,' she says, glaring at me briefly before sucking in some more smoke. Alice is practically purring with satisfaction now, believing herself to have scored a hit.

'Haven't you spent the last decade pretending you're a school-girl in the 1930s?' I say. 'Or are you the schoolmistress? I can see why you wouldn't want to mix with perverts.'

'I'm here on business. If I had known they would be playing *jungle* music at this volume I never would have come.'

She is not referring to a genre of dance music here. To Alice, anything that isn't composed by Germans and played by nice people in dinner jackets fronted by a man waving a white stick is jungle music. She gives the fat man another kick.

'All men are the same,' she says. 'You're no better than him.'

Her voice is practically cracking under the weight of hatred. Sasha would normally be watching the stage show, which is now a display of a willing female slave being fitted into a complex metal gyroscope that will soon whirl her around at high speed, but she is waiting to see what I am going to do about this.

'Keep kidding yourself you just do it for the money,' I say.

Her eyes narrow momentarily. 'I'm not taking that from a pimp!' she says.

Now I don't like that kind of talk. I'm a personal therapist's agent. An entrepreneur. A bodyguard. And quite often the personal therapist's personal therapist. Pimp sounds wrong, to me at any rate.

'Unlike you, I'm not even in the sex industry,' I say.

'How much do you think you would make if you were?' she says.

'More than a piebald, old hag like you,' I reply, and I had been working on that one ever since I noticed it was her. Before this can get worse, Sasha is there with her claws unsheathed.

'What's your problem,' she says to Alice, 'you wrinkly old prune?'

And hello to you too. Have we been introduced? Alice's saggy face just about falls off at that. When she's got everything back where it was and stopped gasping for breath, she sees that Sasha is bouncing up and down on her Docs, grinning in a way that is less than benign. Alice tries a glacial dismissive look, which should work as she's much taller than my little Jack Russell, but it soon crumbles.

'You must be a whore,' says Alice.

'Better than being a dried-up old bag,' says Sasha, hoiking up a big grey-black gobbet of London sputum and planting it halfway up Alice's cheek. Alice maintains her pose of glacial superiority as the oyster-sized nugget slides very slowly down her lined face before it drops to the floor. The sight of a nude fifty-year-old man slithering over to lick this up is not seemly. Fortunately all eyes are on the two contenders as they shape up to each other.

Sasha wrenches her fingers into a shape some might think appropriate to casting a shadow of a little bunny rabbit. It is, of course, a very frightening runic curse, if you were keeping up on ancient Nordic finger insults. Alice is somehow aware that harm is intended and that a reply is required. She leans down towards Sasha then attempts to stub her cigarette out on her face. Before this can happen her hand is batted out of the way by Sasha, who spits quickly upwards in her opponent's face. While Alice goes into a bit of a flap about that, Sasha puts one foot in front of the other and manages to punch Alice hard in the stomach with an efficient straight arm strike. The sound she makes while she does this is meant to harness qi force and punch a hole through a brick wall or something, but it still sounds cute to me. Alice straightens up with some difficulty, then they engage in the sort of comedic flailing that Hollywood used to find amusing before they started pretending that untrained women could punch people without breaking their fingers.

There is a few seconds of this handbags at twenty paces stuff, open-handed slapping and mistimed kicks before they get a grip of each other again. Surprisingly, Sasha goes for the knee in the crotch but doesn't connect as Alice claws her cheek with her crimson fingernails. The volume and pitch of squealing goes up a notch as Sasha copes with the sort of body modification she could have done without. Everyone is watching now as they spit, curse and shriek at each other.

There is a small but persistent market in videos of fighting women, but this does not look like those red-faced American college girls mussing each other's blonde hair and squeezing each other tightly. It looks more like a video made by animal rights activists of an illegal dogfight between two Rottweilers. The fur really is flying now as they sink their teeth into each other. As soon as Alice manages to push Sasha to the floor and straddle her I have to drag her off.

Without a moment's pause for thought, she lunges at me before I can push her away. Sasha kicks her hard in the shins with her fluorescent silver boots. Even now, hopping around on one leg, Alice is trying to jab Sasha in the eye with her long fingernails. Trying not to think about knives, I step between them again without a clear idea of what I'm doing. I have smoked so much skunk recently that even standing up makes me feel tired. I don't even want to win, but once Alice's pointy little teeth have sunk into my hand and she has got several kicks in I feel it is now permissible to chop her throat. I miss and jab her collarbone, which hurts both of us. Sasha looks demented as she hurls herself at Alice. Right now, only bullets will stop her. That or telling her she's starting to look like her mother. Despite this ferocious attack, Alice still manages to throw her across the room, which means I'm supposed to do something again.

While I'm trying to sort out whether it is morally justified to chin Alice, Cathy enters, which makes me hesitate. Alice uses the pause to try to shatter my kneecap with a kick that lands on my upper shin. After a bit of a hobble I lumber back in and get behind Alice, dragging her backwards by her elbows. In my copy of the script she was supposed to be pinioned in my arms while Sasha remonstrated with her. Sasha was supposed to jump up and get a few punches in, then we would walk off hand in hand to make passionate love.

What actually happens is that Alice slips easily out of my grip and nearly claws my eyeball out while Sasha scrabbles ineffectually at her from the floor. Because Cathy is watching, I don't punch or kick Alice, which leaves her a space to try again. She is hissing as she throws herself at me, but just then Cathy steps in quickly with some fancy footwork. She gets a proper choke-hold on Alice, who tries to stamp on Cathy's feet until she blocks off her windpipe. Nothing much happens apart from a savage gloating joy infusing every cell of my body until Alice's eyes start to roll up inside her head.

'Please calm down,' says Cathy, not even out of breath. It's hard not to notice her glossy purple boots, which stretch a long way upwards to where a few inches of Mocchaccino thigh show before her mini-skirt takes over. I probably shouldn't be concentrating on that, and that's definitely what Sasha is trying to tell me with the quick astral head-butt she throws at me when I look guiltily over at her.

'Wow! Where did you learn to do that?' I ask Cathy, and Sasha can fume all she likes; *she* couldn't do it.

'I do some martial arts,' is all Cathy will say.

'What do we do now?' I ask.

'You're the man,' says Sasha, and there just may be a touch of irony here. Someone has dripped vitriol all over the floor anyway. 'Why don't *you* decide?'

'Can I be of assistance, mistress?' says Hugh, who has changed into a rubber bodysuit topped with a round rubber mask that makes him look like a teated condom. Thank God/Odin/My

Lord Lucifer/insert deity of your choice for Hugh. There is someone even I can pity.

It's hard to judge what a man in a black rubber mask is thinking, but his head is lolling on his chest and his voice is barely above a whisper. It's also hard for him to kowtow to Sasha while suggesting simultaneously that I am beneath contempt, but he manages somehow. He hates me for lots of different reasons, but chiefly because I don't want to wrap him in clingfilm and jump up and down on his pinioned packet. I'm a spoilsport. Or repressing my real desires, as he is always trying to suggest.

'Come now, ladies,' he says. 'We are here to enjoy ourselves.'

Hearing the word 'ladies' I instinctively cover my nuts, but everyone ignores Hugh. Alice soon runs out of energy, and after Cathy releases her she goes out to retouch her make-up.

'There's a strange dynamic between you two. Why won't you tell me what it is?' says Sasha.

'Just bad chemistry,' I shrug. Sasha looks at me for a long time – she knows I am lying – but then she blinks a couple of times and says, 'Let's go home.'

Only falling to my knees and kissing her boots could adequately express my gratitude, but it might be misinterpreted in these surroundings. I reach for the keys of the clapped-out London taxi we inherited with our squatted council flat.

Soon we will be tucked up somewhere safe and warm. If the Dungeonmaster's Apprentice isn't lying in wait for us. Or if he hasn't torched the place (what if it's a she? Sasha would say). Or maybe he will do it while we are asleep. Or maybe . . .

'Come on then,' says Sasha. 'What are you waiting for? Cathy's coming too.'

6

IT TURNS OUT that Cathy needs ten more minutes, which probably means half an hour, and I would rather drag Sasha away from here right now before she can talk any more nonsense about 'kicking Alice's butt'. A glance over my shoulder tells me that Alice is still purring malevolence in our direction, but I haven't got time to worry about that because Sasha is snapping at my ankles again.

'Just how did you two meet?' she says, giving Alice the finger as she does so. Hugh puts his arm around Alice and gently steers her away before it can all go off again. 'And why do you hate each other so much?' says Sasha.

'I'm not sure,' I say.

Well, I'm not going to tell her about me and Alice because even now, after about twenty years or so, I still feel guilty. The only consolation is that she would not dare to let the cat out of the bag either. It really wouldn't do either of us any favours.

Suddenly, and typically, Sasha's mood vanishes, to be replaced by something completely unexpected. She grabs hold of my leather jacket, pulls me down to where she is and smothers me with kisses while pummelling her fists against my chest. By the time she has tweaked my nipple and scrotum rings, filled my nostrils with her hot sweet breath and moaned in my ear, I want to take this further. Much further. While I'm busy kneading her body and slobbering nonsense, she whispers, 'Let's do it in one of Maurice's cabinets.' Why not indeed? On the top floor there is no one else around, which may disappoint Sasha, but I feel it's better to make love in private. Hopelessly conservative, but there it is. We scamper up several flights of stairs, laughing as we go, till we find the darkened play area where several restraint cubicles are waiting.

Sasha has that impish look that often presages some startling new innovation in human intimacy and, what with Cathy's smile and sly air of mystery contributing to the general air of fun and frivolity, I am feeling pretty good for once as I step into the cabinet. But instead of soft caresses and the slither of discarded underwear, I hear the door slamming shut, the clank of heavy metal bolts sliding home and an outbreak of crone-like cackling.

Very funny. *Most* amusing.

'I'll let you out when you tell me about you and Alice,' she says, and then there is just footsteps and silence. And the all enveloping thump and clatter of dance music.

Rattling the door only tells me what I already know in my bones: a padlock has been slipped through the hasp.

I still hear feline giggling as I sit down to ponder the situation. My backache reminds me of the afternoon we spent tied to crucifixes in the basement of Rob Power's country residence. We managed to escape that particular predicament, so it's not too hard to be philosophical about this one. After all, Rob was a homicidal maniac and Sasha is the light of my life. There is a difference – at least, there is after I have told myself that salient fact several times, calmly and slowly. Then and only then do I begin to panic.

I was never any good at confinement scenarios. It's not just the immediate predicament; it's what might happen. What if there's a fire? What if nobody knows you are there? What if they forget and you run out of oxygen, which happens often enough as any coroner will tell you?

For a while nothing is happening except the music seems to be getting louder and faster. I wonder whether Sasha will be fucking Cathy somewhere close, and after more time has passed in not entirely unenjoyable conjecture I start to feel very relaxed. Perhaps that's why overworked businessmen like being swaddled in Sellotape and hung from the ceiling. I have no responsibilities. I cannot be reached by fax, telephone or e-mail. Sasha is still coming through loud and clear, although she can't hear my urgent request to get back here and open the door. Or perhaps she's ignoring it. She's like that sometimes.

Just as I'm considering taking forty winks – it's been a long day and it must be getting close to dawn – I hear footsteps and excited chatter, Sasha saying something about me which posterity can live without. As the door to the cabinet is opened, I can see that she has Cathy with her. Which, of course, protects Sasha from any retaliation I might have been planning.

'I'm sorry, I'm sorry,' says Sasha, trying not to laugh as I sit there trying not to hit her.

'We need a lift home. Cathy's dying to see your cab.'

'We will discuss this later, dear,' I say.

'I hope so,' she says, and gives me a special wink which means there might be some punitive fun to be had later. Which sort of makes up for it, but not quite. As does Cathy's whoop of joy on seeing our black cab waiting for her in the deserted street outside.

It's still dark as we get into the cab. The market stalls are still covered, a fox walks nonchalantly down the street in search of discarded fast food, and night buses hurtle past Waterloo with their cargoes of confused drunks and exhausted clubbers.

'Don't you lock it?' says Cathy.

'We don't have the key,' says Sasha. 'Besides, there's nothing to steal. It's just a cab. A stinky old cab full of diesel fumes.'

'Now, now,' I say. 'You know she's easily hurt.'

That gives Sasha the chance to chatter happily about the name we gave her: Astrid, since you ask. I should be watching the road more than I am, but it's hard not to keep looking in the mirror. Sasha and Cathy are seated very close together in very similar postures. 'This is so beautiful,' says Cathy. She is looking at the Imperial War Museum, the dome of which is a feeble echo of St Paul's Cathedral across the river.

'They used to chain mad people up there and poke sticks at them,' says Sasha. 'Rich people used to pay to watch. It was a great night out. When it was Bedlam.'

'Sounds like a good theme, and location, for Richard's next party,' I say.

'I thought Bedlam was somewhere in the East End,' says Cathy, with a lot of confidence considering we live here and she doesn't. Bloody foreigner.

'That was later. It moved,' I add. Nothing disturbs the smooth serene waters of her big brown eyes. She either doesn't believe me or she doesn't care, and how am I supposed to know what she is thinking anyway? Cathy can see what *I'm* thinking, though. I'm annoyed, as I generally am most of the time I'm awake.

'I just love this cab!' she says, beaming beautifully. 'It's really cool.'

I shrug modestly as if we didn't just inherit it with our flat.

'It's a great vehicle for hanging about without attracting attention,' I say.

'Buying drugs,' translates Sasha.

'And taking them,' I say.

Not knowing how well they know each other, I don't say that it is also a perfect vehicle in which to wait for Sasha to complete some business at a punter's place. We soon discovered that it's usually better for me to wait in the cab, as some men find that the appearance of a tattooed shaven-headed thug puts them off l'amour.

'I want a cab too!' says Cathy. 'Are they expensive?'

'Yeah, well. You've got to do the knowledge, darling.'

Cathy looks blank.

'The knowledge!' snorts Sasha, who hates cab drivers and I can't say I blame her. 'The ignorance, more like.'

'You ever see those guys on mopeds reading from clipboards propped up on the handlebars?' I say to Cathy. 'They are training to be cabbies.'

'They're supposed to be learning the quickest routes through London,' butts in Sasha before I can finish this well-worn little jest. 'What they're really learning is the fascist rant they all give you as soon as you get in the cab.'

She does her ape face and switches to a Cro-Magnon version of cockney that is quite unfair to the average cab driver. It's not nearly moronic enough.

'You don't get mini-cabs do yer, darlin'? They're all rapists. They all sign on too, you know. Well, they shouldn't have been let in the country in the first place if you ask me.'

The sound of Cathy's tinkling laughter gently tickles the inside of my ear before settling somewhere deep inside my heart. Grow up, I tell myself. You are spoken for.

'Women drivers!' I shout suddenly at the car in front, as the spirit of the original cab owner claims me.

'Don't *you* start!' says Sasha, her face poking through the little sliding window. She doesn't like being upstaged. I look in the mirror to see that she is holding out an emphatic palm towards me. I know very well this means 'shut up now' but I can't. Not just yet. I reach under the seat and find the flat tweed cap I bought from a charity shop. Sasha starts to shriek.

'Orl right, darlin',' I say.

Sasha starts to beat at the partition with her tiny fists. 'Stop it! Stop it!' she yells, looking quite demented.

'If you ask me,' I say, 'as well as doing the driving test they should make everyone do the knowledge. Then everyone would know the right way. It's obvious really.'

Sasha has her fingers in her ears and is singing loudly while Cathy is still giggling, all sparkly eyes and demure little hand over her mouth, from which high-pitched little squeaks are escaping. This is already one of the memories I would take to a desert island with me along with the time I killed Jason Skinner's brother with one punch. Well, actually that was the time he killed himself by banging his head on the floor, and I don't remember it anyway, but then I will always have the guy I did sober. That still gives me a buzz, and for Sasha's sake I should add the first time we met, and so on and so forth, but that goes without saying. Doesn't it, dear?

I take the cap off and put it under the seat next to my cosh, resolving to buy a big horrible blue nylon anorak to go with it. Sasha and Cathy are huddled together now, knee to knee, talking and laughing loudly about something that doesn't concern me.

First light over the Elephant and Castle brings with it a slight lift to the spirits but also highlights the idiocy of whoever decided to paint the shopping centre pink. It is not a pleasant or uplifting pink either; this is more like the chemically dyed icing on the sort of cakes that only the English would want to eat. We pass the unmemorable memorial to Thomas Edison in the middle of the roundabout, the small silver building which looks like a sci-fi public toilet.

'You live here?' Cathy is asking. 'What does it mean? The Elephant and Castle?'

As Sasha looks blank I seize this opportunity to download some stuff I thought no one would ever want to know. 'It might be because some trading company with Indian connections once had an elephant and castle as a trademark, or it might be because of a Spanish princess called the Infanta of Castille,' I say.

Cathy is still looking in the mirror, but I have lost Sasha already. 'No one knows and no one cares,' she sums up, staring out at a housing estate that would have been considered unacceptably bleak and utilitarian in East Germany.

'You know cockney rhyming slang?' she says, brightening suddenly. 'This one really fits. Elephant and Castle, Asshole. It's the asshole of London.'

It really is looking that way as we park outside our grimy old council estate.

As we enter the communal stairwell of our block of flats, three floors' worth of municipal drabness which are part of a long terraced block, we hear loud hammering. Anywhere else you would have to wonder about someone banging nails into wood with a heavy hammer round about dawn, but most people who live on this estate are nuts. And if they aren't when they move in, they soon will be.

As we make our way upwards it soon becomes clear that the noise is coming from the third floor, where we live. I start to consider that it could be some local teenager attempting a break-in and that remonstrating with him would be the perfect way to work off some of the frustrations of the night. Then I remember the Dungeonmaster's Apprentice and yesterday's little present. I probably should be running away at this point, but as I have foolishly taken the lead up the stairs there is no way out.

'Careful!' shouts Sasha as I take the remaining flights of stairs in a hurry, my heavy boots clattering away almost as loudly as the blood thundering through my eardrums. By the time I have rounded the last stairwell it's hardly a secret that I am approaching our flat. I just catch sight of a bald head, a wispy goatee beard and a hand tattooed with some swirling Celtic shape before the sight of a skinned cat nailed to a crucifix on our door stops me in my tracks. It's not a pretty sight, though I've seen worse, sometimes perpetrated by Sasha in the name of art. As I start to run up the flight of stairs to the communal roof, my heart decides to experiment with a new beat that strongly resembles the sudden rush of metallic percussion on the sort of dance track tailor-made for crackheads. It vanishes as quickly as it started, but it's enough to slow me to a crawl for the remaining stairs. Up on the roof I can see only a distant glimpse of a shaven bald head, a green combat jacket, blue jeans and big boots. He jumps the gap between us and the next block and then carries on running for another fifty yards or so before disappearing down some stairs. I could try to catch him down on the street or I could amble back to the relative safety of our flat and have a nice sit-down and a cup of tea, which is what I decide to do.

While the tea is brewing I wonder whether this might have anything to do with the guy who gave us the keys to this flat. We are presently squat-sitting, not one of Sasha's Tantric exercises but rather we are defending this flat on the Gordon Estate from the council and anyone else who feels they might have a claim to it. The previous tenant has gone on a long tour with a salsa band, which means he will be spending the next six months staring at several pairs of glistening brown female buttocks undulating gracefully and occasionally feverishly as the evening roars to a climax. When he gets back he will be fluent in Portuguese, have repetitive strain injury from hammering away at his piano keyboard four hours a night and will have lost some more of his hearing. They have four timbal players, Yes, four. You can achieve the same sonic holocaust with a sledgehammer on a tin roof, but they claim to be able to tell the difference.

'Did you see who it was?' says Sasha once I'm slumped at the kitchen table waiting for the kettle to boil. She is wide-eyed and breathless as she scrubs her hands clean of the cat's blood. The crucifix is on the table close to where Cathy is sitting, far too calmly for my liking. I didn't exactly expect her to be looking at me with big, frightened eyes and simpering, but neither did I expect quite this air of Zen tranquillity.

'It was a bald guy,' I say. 'With big boots and an army surplus jacket.'

'Oh, well, that narrows it down a bit,' says Sasha, who then catches sight of my face. 'Sorry, it was really great you chased him away.'

And you could make that sound a little more convincing, dearest, but I don't say that because I'm too busy looking at the cat's remains in the bin. Just where I am standing is a glistening little puddle of dark blood, which clashes with my shiny red Dr Martens. The shoes look great, everyone says so, but their bright crimson is no match for the dark lustrous majesty of real blood. If I had better excuses to do so I would spill that stuff more often just to watch it shine. But enough of my hobbies.

'It's probably something to do with the guy whose flat this is,' I say to Cathy. 'I wouldn't worry about it.'

If only she would look worried. Or cared what I was saying.

She's just staring at Sasha waiting for her to tell us what's really happening.

'I'm not worried about it,' says Sasha. 'I just want to know who it is. A bald guy. He could be a gay skinhead, a New Age skinhead, a real skinhead, if there are any left in London . . .'

'A middle-aged man worried about male pattern baldness,' I say, 'or a Hare Krishna who has lost his ponytail in a freak shaving accident.'

'Or a lesbian into s/m . . .'

'I'm going to bed,' I announce but then see a quick flicker pass between Sasha and Cathy. They avoid my eyes. Which would seem to indicate that they have something considerably more stimulating in mind than reading Jane Austen while sipping Earl Grey tea.

Trying not to kick anything, I blunder into the bathroom, where I notice I have aged some five hundred years or so. Sasha joins me and yanks her pants down before slowly peeling off the polythene covering on her fresh tattoo. She gets some cream out of a jar and rubs it very gently into the fresh multicoloured carving on her bottom. For a few days the new tattoo will look glossy and shiny, then she will need the patience of Job not to pick at the scab and let it fall off naturally, after which it will gradually unveil itself slightly duller than its present hyper-real colours. She sighs softly as she peels back the polythene wrapping from her wounded flesh. Her mouth forms into an overdone O of surprise that she overuses if you ask me. She knows it always gets the crowd going, but I doubt if her heart is in it right now. Not with Cathy on the premises.

'I'm going up on the roof,' I say, trying not to sulk too much.

Sasha brightens up considerably before she remembers she's supposed to look disappointed that I'm taking my leave. I nod sourly to her then look in to see that Cathy is engrossed in something on the table, a note Sasha left for me. This is one of her elaborate little jests, a quiz written the way it might look in a glossy consumer magazine with some appropriate illustrations glued into place. Underneath the title 'Are You a Serial Killer?' is one of our photobooth portraits, not the lovey-dovey one we do every year on our anniversary but one of the ones where we smear our faces with fake blood and bare our teeth in a grim rictus of death. Underneath this are a number of questions, such as Are you tattooed? Do you indulge in perverse sexual practices? Were you abused as a child? Do you hate authority? Do you have violent mood swings? Do you suffer from depression or any other long-term mental disorder? To nearly all of these questions Sasha has added two ticks, one for her and one for me. There is only one missing; I can't claim to have been abused. The quiz made me laugh this morning, but it's probably not the sort of joke that should be shared with guests.

As it happens, we do fit the profile that lazy forensic psychiatrists make up, and we have helped a few people over to the other side, as it were, but it wasn't our fault. They started it. They did. It's never us. Anyway, Cathy is lapping it up, head bent to the paper, eyes greedily hoovering up the information. Maybe she is trying to evaluate Sasha's crabbed and skewed handwriting, also proof positive of every type of psychosis imaginable.

'Nothing like our great British sense of humour,' I say, rubbing my hands together and plastering an idiotic grin on my face.

It isn't even fooling me.

Cathy looks right through me for a few seconds while a little sprite whispers in my ear: 'She knows all about you, mate.'

But then I know all about her and that bloodsucking business so maybe it's a draw.

'I'm just going up on the roof for some fresh air,' I say, already feeling an intruder in my own house. There is a nod and a genuine smile, but what it all means is open to question. The strongest contender would seem to be: 'Thanks for being so considerate. Now nob off and let us get down to it.'

I really can't face listening to those two making love. Well, I could under different circumstances, but right now I don't fancy either ruining their fun or trying to sleep on the couch while a chorus of Tantric screeching emanates from next door. I might as well watch the weak autumnal sun rise over Central London rather than hang about down here. It will be a good chance to get used to being alone.

7

IT'S 6 A.M. but I know I won't sleep. One of the grubby, white-faced clowns from the anarchist food collective appears, dreadlocks waving in the wind. He starts to prat about on one leg while waving his hands in the air. I consider asking him why his tins of sugarless baked beans cost one pound each or why all of his serving staff smoke toxic little roll-ups while preaching at you or why they all smell strongly of sweat, but I'm too tired even to take a pop at him.

Just as I wearily close my eyes an outburst of female whooping from downstairs confirms my worst fears. Shortly after, I recognise Sasha's heavy boots clumping up the stairs. It would seem we have some good news.

'Richard called me!' she says, shaking me like a toddler waking up a half-dead parent. 'Hugh is staging one of his special scenes! He wants all of us there. We get a grand each. But it has to be now!'

'Special scenes?'

'You know.'

I do know, of course. I was just contemplating whether I have the energy to watch Hugh being subjected to some lewd life-threatening torture at a time when the citizens are tucking into their muesli. 'Might this involve some *hanging* around?' I say.

She has heard this one before but manages a weak smile anyway. '*Such* a clever boy,' she says.

I can't say I'm pleased. Autoerotic strangulation before break-fast doesn't really do it for me. I look over at the dome of St Paul's rather than at Sasha. It doesn't dampen her enthusiasm.

It's a good time to be up here before the other t'ai chi hippies start their silly hopping about, also while there is still something close to silence, before Sasha and Cathy really get going. As I lie down on an old mattress I remember that a couple making love was supposedly one of the sounds Duke Ellington was trying to evoke in a piece called 'In a Harlem Airshaft'. If it was called that and if some band member or Billy Strayhorn didn't write it anyway. Look, I don't care, they're all dead now, and I'm willing to bet it sounded nothing like a Harlem airshaft anyway. The point is, or will be when I get to it, that if you are going to write a tone poem called 'On the Roof of Our Estate at the Elephant and Castle' you are going to need a lot more than some strident lovemaking to paint a realistic picture.

Over the backwash of non-stop traffic there should be some police sirens and, very occasionally, some realistic gunfire. Not too far away is the sort of villains' pub where feuds stretching back generations are occasionally settled with a shot in the back. Don't forget to duck if you hear anything untoward while ordering your mild and bitter. You will also need three different unsynchronised sources of current dance music and some acoustic folk played by unwashed white men with dreadlocks. For maximum authenticity they should have been to a public school and also fancy themselves as clowns, jugglers or fire-eaters. An optional extra for Sasha and me is the man directly below us who spends a great deal of time shouting very loudly at someone who may be his wife. During the hours of darkness, he practises reggae DJ-ing, which I believe was once called toasting. He mikes himself up to achieve the unusual feat of being deafening yet incomprehensible, and Sasha won't let me say the rest of what I think about that.

'Come on!'

'Why would you trust him? About the money?'

'You know he always pays cash. You can get some toot off Richard. And it's something to do with the Black Order. We could join if this works out. Come on!'

She's jumping up and down now. Lately she has been banging on incessantly about this secret society of highly dubious self-styled sorcerers.

'I'm sick of people like Richard and their pathetic attempts to be the next Aleister Crowley,' I say. 'It's just an excuse to take enormous amounts of drugs and have twisted sex with as many brain-dead disciples as they can muster.'

Put that way, it doesn't sound so bad, but anything to do with Richard is likely to involve some highly non-consensual sex strapped to his Black and Decker workmate. Even t'ai chi is better than that.

'Don't pretend you're not interested,' says Sasha. 'His gang is like your Black Church of Eternal Hellfire was. Except successful. We could even take it over.'

'You don't take over a cult.'

A big beaming smile tells me that Sasha thinks you can. She probably could too, if her old man wasn't hobbling along behind her, gagging for a mug of decaff and looking for a comfortable settee to read the paper on.

'Cathy's coming,' she says slyly.

'Really? Well, let's not keep Queen Cathy waiting.'

She doesn't bother replying as I raise my creaking body off the coffee-stained mattress. Free drugs and money. It could, after all, be worse. Not that that will ever stop me complaining.

'It has to be now,' I say. 'Typical whining submissive. Just to prove he can boss us around.'

'Just think of the money,' she says.

'You're going native,' I tell her. She looks blank. 'That's what the local villains always say.'

But she has already clattered back downstairs, having assumed, rightly, that I'm driving them there.

8

'ARE YOU SURE Cathy is ready for this?' I say, while Cathy is in the bathroom.

'She was a hostess. In Hong Kong,' says Sasha.

'Yes. But giving businessmen hand jobs is not quite the same as watching Hugh dangling from the end of a gibbet.'

'You worry too much,' she says, reaching up to kiss me.

In what Sasha and Cathy probably think is a little while later we all get into the cab again and set off for Tribal Tattoos. Cathy now has upward strokes of mascara in the corner of her eyes, a black cashmere sweater, shiny black boots, black seamed nylons and her hair looks 1960s to me, as far as I would know, being a man. She is radiating beauty, intelligence and a certain off-centre quirkiness that the rest of the world considers to be British. Which is all very well, but the wait for last-minute primping and preening has not left me in the best of moods. Or maybe it's the sulphate Sasha has just chopped out or the freshly ground coffee I brewed to put in my Costas Coffee travel mug. Swigging from this black beaker while feeling the fire in my veins from the sulphate leaves me in no mood for incoming gibberish. Even if it's from Cathy.

'You just *have* to live in London,' Cathy is saying.

I have heard and read this so often now I have to say something. Even if it might contradict Cathy. 'Yes, who can resist Swinging London? We have the thinnest, dopiest-looking models. They take the most drugs and smoke the most cigarettes. Which certainly puts Renaissance Italy in its place. Leonardo da Vinci? Just how thin was he? We have pop groups who nearly sound like the Beatles would have done if they had never read any books or been to school. Drugs? Get your toot here, guaranteed cocaine-free. Why bother with the loved-up feeling you get from MDMA when you can spend fifteen quid on speed and caffeine. Culture? Let Nick Hornby explain why thick yobs kicking each other is supposed to be interesting.'

'Have some more grump juice, Matt,' says Sasha, which is her way of reminding me I've had too much coffee.

'I will, thank you,' I say, slopping some over the side of the mug as I drive one-handed.

'He's a hopeless addict,' says Sasha, with an affectionate smile. Least, I hope that is what that face means. It might just as well mean pity rather than affection. The sort of pity people feel when they have decided to leave someone.

'It's always been like this anyway,' says Sasha. Even when she's agreeing with me she has to turn it into an argument somehow. 'Read Smollett.'

'What?'

'He does three pages on how crowded, noisy and smelly London is, how the food is adulterated, how the inhabitants are either noisy hooligans or snobby posers. I mean, has anything changed since the late eighteenth century? Except we now have fake drugs to go with the fake food and the fake beer. And noise he couldn't possibly have imagined.'

And the colonies became some place called America, which later spawned a little demon with a penchant for murdering husbands past their sell-by date. Which reminds me that we have been together for twice as long as her last marriage. Perhaps I should make a will.

As we arrive at the deserted office Richard throws us down the keys from the third floor. The scene will apparently take place in the top-floor office, an area that was locked last night. When we get up there it's hard to avoid noticing that Hugh is naked except for a noose – a real one that works – and tight black rubber pants. Richard is wearing green combat trousers. This has nothing to do with the brief fashion fad for such items; he is obsessed with militaria, preferably German, needless to say. His upper body is scored with fresh lacerations and he looks quite insane, eyes rolling around his head and lower jaw working away constantly. Hugh and Richard are both covered in sweat. Even Stanley the Rhodesian Ridgeback looks wired, straining at his leash and barking at his own tail. Even with this to look at, and a full-size gibbet in the far corner, the eye gravitates instantly to an item hung up next to Hugh's boring blue suit and Richard's military casuals. The item in question could be a genuine SS uniform, knowing Richard, but a fake is no less offensive, even to a party of people who have taken class-A drugs to enable them to assist in erotic strangulation at 8.30 a.m. on a Sunday morning. Sasha is staring intently at the shiny black-peaked cap, the razor-edge creases, the faded badges and above all the black backcloth of the jacket on which two silver sun runes twinkle. I know she would love one of these alluring little items, but whether they made them for persons of restricted growth is another matter.

'Wow,' she says finally. At least she didn't say 'cool', but it wasn't far off.

'Ye-e-es,' drawls Richard, drawn over to salivate along with us. 'Black has hypnotised human beings ever since they could tell the difference between day and night.'

He strokes the armband. 'Red for blood!' Here he looks at me, and when he gets bored with waiting for me to look away he continues: 'Silver for the moon, the unconscious, the feminine. Evil itself!'

Sasha stifles a yawn then opens her little black bag and affixes a number of clothes pegs to Hugh's scrotum. He doesn't appear to notice but she's still warming up. Cathy is concentrating on the full-sized gallows, while I am trying to work out what she is thinking without being caught staring at her yet again.

'Can you get my mask?' says Hugh, to me. 'It's in my briefcase.'

I stand there staring at him. 'I am not part of the service industry, Hugh. You know this.'

'You have been hired for the day,' Hugh says. 'Unless you want to give me the money back.'

'Hugh, I don't ever "give the money back".'

Such a challenge to the only thing I really believe in – apart from you, Sasha – requires the eyeball screw. I give him a good drilling, but he still has a little smirk that needs erasing.

'We operate a strictly cash upfront, no-guarantee, no-money-back service,' I say.

'Fine,' says Hugh. 'But you could walk downstairs and get my mask. That's not too much trouble for a thousand pounds, is it?'

I'm about to tell Hugh where he can stick his thousand pounds when Sasha catches my eye. He is our best client, after all. I go and find his box of tricks, inside which is a black gas mask with a long breathing tube attached.

These presently modish items are much in demand when

utilised by rubber-clad women, especially when the other end of the breathing apparatus is plugged into what Taoists call the Jade Gate. I dread to think where Hugh might stick the other end of this thing, but I hand him the mask and sit down once more. At least it muffles his voice, but I can still hear him all too well.

'Are you still pretending you don't like hanging?' he is saying, having latched on to me because he can see I don't want him to.

I shrug. 'As they say on the net, YKIOKIJNMK.' I had to close my eyes and speak slowly so as not to fuck up the acronym, and as I open them again Richard is sneering and Sasha is still staring at the floor.

'Your kink is OK; it's just not my kink,' says Richard, who has to remind us he knows more about pervery than anyone else in the whole world ever.

'It's hardly a "kink",' says Hugh, feathers all ruffled.

'Well . . .'

'You're supposed to be open-minded and you're trying to define me as some sort of a pervert.'

'But . . .'

'It's not as if your little frolics with blood are any safer, is it?'

I look at Sasha, who is all of a sudden occupied with retying the purple laces on her silver knee-length boots. That little peccadillo is supposed to be a secret, one of the things that binds us together in a special way because no one else knows about it. Till now. I wonder if she has told Cathy, who also seems to have a penchant for plasma.

I never heard Hugh laugh before, which would have been odd in itself but it's especially spooky coming all the way down that rubber breathing tube. Richard doesn't like the focus of attention drifting away from him, and it may be this which inspires him to cut the flesh of his belly once more and taste the fresh blood. It may also be because it's a long time past his bedtime.

It was probably him who has painted the mirrored wall with 'Do what thou wilt shall be the whole of the law', perhaps for old time's sake. Aleister Crowley doesn't shock the way he used to – now you can buy all that sex, drugs, astrology and yoga stuff from any high-street bookstore – but the swastikas daubed all around the stage are undoubtedly eye-catching. Sasha certainly thinks so.

'People say you're working for some Nazi occultist now,' she says, glaring up at him.

'People say a lot of things about me,' he says, throwing his arms wide now the spotlight is on him once more. 'But you should know better to believe gossip.'

I remember Sasha saying that this shadowy black magician has an army of slaves and looks on the Second World War as a flawed rehearsal for the deciding conflict that will break out any day soon. But she doesn't know who this guy is, only Richard's initiates know, and you have to join their club to find out.

Telling Sasha she doesn't need to know who it is just hardens her resolve. Ignoring her doesn't work either. But there is no point worrying about her meddling in things that don't concern her until we have strung Hugh up.

'This is disgusting. I don't want to be here,' says Cathy, arms folded across her chest.

'Not you too, sweetie,' says Richard. 'Swastikas are just your basic sun and moon symbols. We are just reclaiming the sunwheel and taking it back to its roots in Atlantis.'

'So why do your followers wear combat gear and have shaven heads?' asks Cathy.

'Because we are the master race,' says Richard, using his ersatz German accent.

'Perhaps it's just living in Hampstead,' I say. 'Waking up looking down on the rest of London.'

'Or perhaps it's because I am ten feet tall and a karate black belt,' says Richard. 'If you want to follow the path of the strong, the first step on the path is to confront your worst fears. You lot can't even cope with a few symbols scrawled on the wall.'

'Do you really collect Nazi memorabilia?' says Sasha.

'I have an extensive collection of uniforms,' he says, 'very few of which are Nazi, but it is surprising how excited people get at the sight of *those* particular items. *Very* excited in some cases.'

Not only is Richard looking at me, but he seems to have turned everyone else's head my way. For once I am innocent, so it is best to ignore this charge. But I have to say something. 'It's usually spotty teenagers who think it's cool to wear Charles Manson T-shirts. Or Nazi uniforms. They usually get over it by fifty.'

As it happens I had rehearsed this bit already for this very eventuality and manage to say it in the right order and at the right speed. Leaving the word fifty till last seemed to me to be the best part of it. How could any gay man recover from that? I had imagined that I might have to defend myself physically, but there isn't even a dent in his smile. The inference is that I just don't matter.

'And the gays who died in the camps?' says Cathy, very calm, very controlled. 'The Gypsies? The Jews?'

Richard shakes his head. 'They make far too much of the Holocaust if you ask me,' he says. 'They were begging for it anyway. Gagging for it, mate.'

'Is that genuine or a fake?' I say, nodding towards the uniform. Richard's smile slips for a millisecond.

'The very fact that you can ask such a question shows how utterly, utterly pedestrian you are. Why are you incapable of serious thought? In the Black Order we experiment with artifice and the construction of reality...'

Richard then talks about some French philosophers whom most people quite rightly haven't heard of while I keep trying not to look at Cathy. I suppose he feels even less inclined to shut up with that uniform in his wardrobe. Finally he finishes off with: ' . . . the Lacanian lack-in-being represented by the erect penis.'

There is a pause for applause that will not be forthcoming from me or anyone else in earshot, but he somehow manages to bask in the afterglow anyway. *He* knows he's right.

'That will be Alice,' he says as the doorbell rings.

Sasha turns bright red, stands up and opens her mouth to start what looks like a long tirade, but before she can launch into whatever she was going to say Hugh holds out a thick wedge of notes to her.

'Come on,' he says, 'I want you to work together.'

Sasha looks like she is going to refuse the money for a moment but then shrugs at me and folds the wad up neatly before putting it in an inaccessible pocket. There is a triumphant glint in Hugh's eyes as he gets to be in control once more, but it seems a pretty pointless, and expensive, sort of victory to me.

'I think I'll change,' says Richard, pirouetting out of the room, probably because no one has been looking at him for a while. Alice eventually arrives, gasping for breath after three flights of stairs, looking even more cadaverous in the unflattering morning light. Like Sasha, she insists on getting paid before anything else happens. Once she has counted her money she passes the gallows without a second glance and sits down on the horrid old sofa as far as she can from the rest of us. Soon she has a protective barrier of smoke going, most of which is drifting towards my lungs. We exchange glares, but that's soon irrelevant for Richard has made an entrance in *that* uniform.

'It's genuine,' he says to Alice, as he stands there preening himself. To watch him whirl through a dizzying succession of over-the-top poses you would think that an enthusiastic photographer was geeing him up every step of the way rather than a wall of silent and sullen opposition.

He grins sardonically as he produces a silver dish of white powder which makes everyone present instantly wish they had been a bit nicer to him. Once this has gone round, there is a frank exchange of views on the uniform issue, but as everyone is talking at once, and it's all been said before, I spend most of the time looking at Cathy. Unfortunately she is always looking at Sasha, but I can dream. Three-quarters of an hour passes with Richard winding us all up something rotten. Then, as the women are occupied prodding Hugh with big sticks, I get the chance to speak to him alone.

'Where did you get the uniform from?' I say, quieter than before but with harder eyes and a lot closer to him than I should be. This isn't really an argument about aesthetics or whatever it is that Richard is talking about; this is about inherited money and those infuriating people who actually like themselves enough to be happy.

'I suppose you would stop scowling at me if I gave you some more cocaine, but why should I?' he says. 'You affect to despise me. Why should I give you my drugs?'

He's got me there. I've gone too far to slip back into coke-whore mode. Which only leaves me the option of trying to achieve some pathetic victory over this Nazi uniforms business, particularly as Sasha and Cathy are looking over now. I might as well get used to saying Sasha and Cathy as they already look like a couple. And not like a couple who bicker about domestic chores or argue in public but like two people who are a long way from slaking their insatiable thirst for each other. Their eyes and teeth are sparkling as they bestow long, lingering looks on each other. Richard is gloating as he watches me suffer, so I clear my throat and have another go at him.

'Leaving aside all that crap about how the SS was the most successful magical sect ever – you just say that to shock people – doesn't the Holocaust ever make you feel guilty?'

'The Holocaust? Wasn't that on the telly? The musical version? I remember the songs now . . . "Send in the Kleins" . . .'

'You bastard!' Sasha is screaming at him now, although there are moments in her past when she has flirted with the imagery of fascism. This was never done to get her picture in the paper, of course. She would never stoop to such tactics. She only ever posed half-naked wearing a Stormtrooper's cap just to open the debate on transgressive images of women. We were still in New York then, and when an orthodox Jew turned up as a client asking her to wear 'that uniform' she couldn't cope, and I can't say I blame her. She tried saying she only worked Saturdays but that just made him keener. Let's move on. Sasha is still raving away at Richard.

'How can you, as a gay man, justify flirting with images of oppression? The Nazis hated gays.'

'I'm not gay, I'm queer, dear. And as for the Nazis "hating gays", who do you think designed the uniforms? And the Nuremberg rallies? And the light shows?'

My heart sinks as Cathy starts to talk seriously about Jacques Derrida. Just as I'm starting to reassess my desire for Cathy in the light of this dreadful revelation, Sasha motions me over.

'He fucks that dog of his,' she says, for once looking as mad and angry as I often do.

'I thought Stanley was walking with a pronounced limp.'

'Shut up! Hugh told me.'

'No, I didn't.'

'Shut up! Shut up!'

She looks at me until I bow my head slightly to signify she is still the top dog. As if we were in any doubt. 'He says that as we share ninety-eight per cent of our DNA with animals and they consent to it there is nothing wrong.'

'Can't see it convincing the judge myself,' I say, until I realise I'm supposed to be denouncing Richard in the sort of fire-and-brimstone language that priests and the police usually reserve for Sasha herself. I had heard rumours that Richard knows a lot about the sexual responses of horses in particular and regularly posts advice on the Internet, most of which goes a lot further than 'You need a stool to stand on'.

Sasha is tapping her foot and assuming various attack postures while failing to organise whatever it is she is trying to say. This is condition red. Time to say something soothing. Or move out. One or the other.

'So it's wrong,' I say. 'Now what? I don't know. Maybe Stanley will bite his knob off one day.'

'Someone certainly should.'

Richard dances over to us, trying not to chew his lips off or let his eyes explode. I want some of what he has just had, but I could never ask without becoming one of his underlings. All of which makes me mad enough to pose this question: 'Richard, you haven't got one of your novices to nail a cat to our door, have you?'

There seems to be genuine surprise in his mad laughter, but how can you tell after the ingestion of a serious amount of chemicals?

'Really?' he says. 'How exciting. Did you eat it?'

'No. And we didn't fuck it either.'

Richard thinks that's very funny, so funny that he is soon wiping the tears from his eyes. 'Wasn't the erotic competition boring?' says Hugh, his sad, dull voice further deadened by the long breathing tube. Normally this remark would be ignored, but as he has just paid out several thousand pounds Sasha manages a barely audible grunt of acknowledgement. 'Nobody seemed to realise that the crucial concept in sex is control and counter-control. The chess game between the dominant and the sub-missive. The balance of power.'

Richard, predictably, is not impressed.

'Really? How dreadfully dreary! I prefer cock myself. As much of it as I can fit up my . . .'

'Be that as it may,' I say. 'This isn't a social occasion.'

'Yeah. Come on, Hugh,' says Richard. 'Let's get you strung up so we can all get home and start spending your money. You pathetic old fart.'

Anxious looks pass between Sasha and I. And everyone who isn't Richard. He might not believe in mollycoddling the paying customer, but we need his money. It's hard to tell what Hugh is thinking underneath the mask, but his belly is rising and falling at a frenetic pace. He gets his briefcase, has a frantic rummage inside it then brings out a handgun – not a revolver but other than that I haven't a clue. It's some time since I flicked through *Guns for Target Shooting and not at all for Shooting People* in W.H. Smith. The point is that he looks very comfortable with the weapon in his hand, and no one is laughing at him now.

'That's a replica,' sneers Richard. 'And I'm going to shove it right up your arse.'

Hugh surprises us all by pointing the gun very carefully at Richard's Ridgeback and holding it steady with both hands, as if he knows what he is doing. The hound is sleeping faithfully by his master, but the shot soon wakes him up. Stanley goes on the attack but can't do much apart from void his bowels and flail his limbs in a spastic dervish dance of rattling bones while whining haplessly. A second shot drops him motionless, silencing him for ever. Although Sasha is still and blank-faced, I can tell that she is feeling more than she ever did watching human beings die.

There is a long silence throughout which we can still hear the echo of the shots. In case you're wondering, the reason why Richard has shut the fuck up for once is that the gun is pointing right at him. There is now a smell of cordite and urine. There is a damp patch on Richard's crotch, and I try not to think about how I would like Cathy to squat over my head and piss all over my face, preferably through a pair of flimsy white knickers I could keep as a souvenir. Then I realise I'm supposed to be thinking up ways to get us out of here, but that's probably best left to Sasha. Or it used to be till Cathy showed up.

'It's not so easy without the dog, is it?' says Hugh, whose quavery high voice would seem to indicate that he is upset about something. There are going to be tears before bedtime. He is standing in front of Richard now, pointing the gun directly at his chest.

'You're not going to shoot,' says Richard, but he doesn't sound so sure.

I can't resist smiling sweetly at Richard. I've waited a long time for this.

'That was for not letting me into the Black Order,' says Hugh, sounding like a four-year-old. No one is in any hurry to point this out presently.

'I'm going to put this gun down now. For all I care you can shoot me with it. I still want to be hanged. And not rescued. And I wanted to see you lot wrestle with your supposed consciences. Whether you would kill someone for a thousand pounds. Or just sit there and watch.' He inclines his head towards Cathy.

'I also want to prove that you should never have looked down on me. You all do, although Sasha and Cathy might pretend not to. To be submissive is to be the stronger half of the s/m power exchange. We take the original childhood trauma and say, "Look, pain doesn't even hurt. Do what you want. I even like it. And I can take more than you can give." '

This is almost certainly the longest speech he has ever been allowed to make in this company. We are all looking grave and respectful, as if he is telling us the secret of the universe. Except Richard.

'If you ever do put that gun down I'm going to kill you,' whispers Richard. 'There will be nothing left of you except a big rubber bag of mangled flesh, crushed bones and teeth.'

Richard is trying to sit still, but under the strain of bottling it up his limbs are twitching and his facial muscles are out of control. Hugh puts the gun down and looks defiantly at Richard. Before he can make good his threats, Sasha picks the weapon up and points it straight at him.

'One word out of you and you're going on those gallows. And we might just forget to cut you down.'

Either she doesn't like Richard's sneery grin or it's the allegations of inappropriate inter-species familiarity that are still riling her – there must be some reason why she suddenly puts a bullet into the couch where Richard is sitting. No one moves for a long time while we look at Sasha, who is holding the weapon very straight indeed, breathing deeply and slowly and focusing on her target to the exclusion of all else. Then Hugh starts to gasp and pant.

'He's coming. Can you believe it?' says Alice. Sasha doesn't turn to look; she is concentrating very hard on Richard. Thankfully, you can't tell if Hugh is coming underneath the rubber pants but the writhing around is very impressive. In fact it's getting annoying, all this leaping around like a freshly landed haddock. It's a relief when his head slumps on to his chest and he goes limp all over. I watch the standoff between Sasha and Richard for a while and then notice that Hugh has yet to move. Surely the old fool hasn't decided to take a quick nap? Not now, with the prospect of a dance with death supervised by Supreme Ogress Sasha about to commence. He looks very peaceful, though; in fact he looks like he may never move again.

'Hugh!' says Sasha, giving him a shake. His body slumps to one side as Richard begins to cackle. She still has the gun; not that she needs it to make us do what she wants.

'Get his mask off,' she says.

Cathy peels the mask off, but it looks like it's too late.

'He's stopped breathing,' she says.

'It worked!' says Richard. 'I willed him to die. And he did! Brilliant! Yes!'

He punches the air with a clenched fist as the rest of us stop panicking for a moment to stare at him. His cruellest smile appears. 'Looks like Sasha got her wish. Remember what she said? She'd like to plug up his airways and watch him die?'

There is a shocked silence as we all look at Sasha, who is looking scared all of a sudden. Cathy looks far too calm, Alice's uptilted chin and cold eyes are still trying to suggest that we shouldn't really be intruding on her presence, and Richard is laughing so hard that he falls to his knees before rolling around pounding the floor with his fists.

9

'I BELIEVE "POOR HUGH" is the appropriate reaction,' I say as soon as Richard stops laughing, which takes a while. Sasha starts to massage Hugh's heart, looking as if she knows what she is doing, although health professionals presumably don't say 'fuck' this often. While that's going on I sit here being as much use as I generally am in a crisis. Richard's contribution is a smirk that I would dearly love to wipe off his face, although any attempt to do so is likely to leave me wherever Hugh is now. Between incarnations. Resting, as actors say.

Cathy is remarkably calm. I know women don't jump up on chairs clutching their skirts at the sight of a mouse any more, but most civilians find a fresh cadaver unsettling, a bit of a conversation stopper. It's making me wonder about what she did before she became a bloodsucking tattooist.

Alice is steely-eyed and silent, anaesthetising herself with a cigarette. She sneers as she catches my eye, each drag of the cigarette punching hollows into her sagging, wrinkly face. As Richard starts skinning one up, Sasha is still pounding away at Hugh's chest with bunched fists. It may be doing her some good, but it's doing absolutely nothing for him.

'He's dead, dear,' says Richard, by the time his joint is ready to light. 'You can jump up and down on him if you like, it won't make any difference.'

'It's certainly made very little difference to you,' I say to Richard.

'Yes, well,' he says, exhaling skunk smoke, and even those two words sting when delivered in his condescending drawl. 'He was a pain when he was alive, and he is going to be a bloody nuisance now he's dead.' Some malevolent inspiration puts one of his nastiest smiles on his face. And he's aiming it straight at me.

'Look! He's balding, like you.' Richard pulls the combed-over hair away from Hugh's bald spot.

'I am proudly shaven,' I say. 'I am not balding.'

'Still not over it, eh? Never mind. At least you have Sasha. Though you don't deserve her.'

He's looking at Sasha now with a predatory gleam in his eye, and my heart sinks at the thought that, as well as Cathy, I might have to compete with a rich guy whose chief virtue is that he isn't me, the person Sasha has already slept next to for far too long. And Sasha was always looking for a real English gentleman, something like Richard or one of the suave sophisticated ones they have in films, not the inbred chinless ditherers or the nasty junkies they tend to have in real life. Sasha just looks straight through him, bless her, but it's one more thing to worry about. Apart from the minor detail of disposing of a very fat man's mortal remains.

'What are we going to do?' says Cathy.

Put another advert in for more punters first thing Monday morning is the first thing to occur to me, but this isn't the right moment. There is a loud long fart from Hugh, excusable in the circumstances.

'He's alive,' says Alice, almost sitting up in her seat.

'Hallelujah!' says Richard, throwing up both arms and capering about in simulated ecstasy.

'It's the death rattle, you silly cow,' says Sasha, but her usual venom is absent. Her eyes are starting to glaze over, the way they do when she sometimes shuts up shop for three days on the run, getting out of bed only to go to the bathroom. Times like that there is nothing to be done except hide the knives and razor blades and make sure she can't get hold of any sleeping tablets.

Just to try to cheer her up I say, 'What would Emma Peel do?'

Cathy lights up. 'You like *The Avengers*! This is my dream! I love them! I want to see all the locations! I want to meet Diana Rigg . . .'

There's more, but I'm too busy cupping my head in my hands to record it. Now there's another reason it's always going to be two against one. Obsessives are supposedly male, as women journalists never tire of telling us, but Cathy and Sasha certainly seem to have got the moves down.

'I like the black and white ones best,' says Sasha, eyes shining. 'I used to watch that stuff and dream about coming to England one day.'

'Me too!' says Cathy, and they hunker down into a serious bonding ritual, chirping and chirruping away long enough to get right on my tits.

' . . . and the "Queen of Sin" episode,' Cathy is saying five minutes later.

' "A Touch of Brimstone",' corrects Sasha, happy that she can display her knowledge.

I have to step in here. 'The snake? And the basque? She

never looked right. You could tell she would rather be doing a Shakespeare matinée. She was always a delight, of course, because she had something you can't fake: poise, charm . . .'

They both turn to look at me then simultaneously turn back and chatter on. I am not John Steed, that is all that needs to be known right now. While they swap trivia, including the episode numbers, for fuck's sake, I ponder briefly on the harem episode where you get to see one millimetre of bottom cheek cleavage in the instant just before Diana Rigg hitches her belly dancer pants back up. The second time Sasha says empowerment I have to step in. 'The men just stand there and let her throw them about. Which is all that happens in Xena, Warrior Princess . . .'

'You want to be thrown around by Diana Rigg. You just don't want to admit it.'

This is to ignore a considerable portion of our private life, but I'm not quite ready to tell Cathy about all that just yet. But does she already know? I feel a bacon sandwich coming on, with plenty of stinging English mustard. It might just match the bitter sting of rejection which is starting to throb uncomfortably. But there is Hugh to dispose of. As Richard points out, now he has rolled another joint.

'I'm assuming no one here wants to phone the police,' he says.

'We all have far too much to lose,' says Cathy. 'We get rid of the body and then we must never speak of these matters again. He must disappear from the face of the earth.'

There is a silence while we get our heads round that one but Richard just has to ruin it. 'Oooh!' he says, standing up and executing a camp twirl. 'Get her. And I thought you were an amateur, dear.'

'Shut up,' she says, betraying no annoyance whatsoever. Exactly the right strategy and one I can never manage myself.

'We all have many reasons why we cannot subject ourselves to investigation by the police,' she says. 'We must now unite.' She looks at Sasha and Alice in turn here. 'It is easy enough to dispose of a body, if we stick together.'

A big if. I look round the room at our little rainbow alliance. It doesn't exactly inspire confidence. I can't even trust Sasha, now that she is likely to be spending the next millennium or so lapping at Cathy's boots.

'We don't even have to dispose of him,' says Richard. 'The safest thing to do is for us all to go over to Hugh's place and dump him there. Before he goes stiff. He will lie there till the neighbours get wind of him. When he starts to smell.'

'Getting him out of here should be easy,' I say, trying to ignore Richard's grin and also keep the edge out of my voice. 'You know how he's always going on about three-day confinement scenarios. We just wrap him up in about sixteen different layers and dump him somewhere. Who's going to investigate a bondage accident?'

Even Richard can't criticise this. Sasha just has to though, probably because I said it. 'There were a lot of potential witnesses here last night,' she says.

'Yes. They may remember you threatening to kill him, dear,' says Richard spitefully.

'The coroner will just say he had a heart attack during one of his games,' I say quickly, trying to erase Richard's last comment. 'He's written about it often enough. "How I love messing around in the mud with nasty rough men." '

'It was actually "Confinement Scenarios in the Open Air",' says Richard, too scornfully for my taste.

'Well, excuse me!'

'Oh, who cares?' says Richard. 'Let's get this loser out of the way and then go and get wasted.'

'You're all heart,' I say.

'You fucking hypocrite.' Richard's eyes are starting to blaze again. 'Don't you dare look at me like that! You never liked him and, let's face it, he's going to be much happier under the ground than he ever was above it. Surely burial is the ultimate confinement scenario for a bondage freak.'

Richard is now looking at four hostile faces, but he isn't going to let a difficult audience get to him.

'In the aftermath of orgasm Hugh closed his eyes and slumped to the floor, for all the world as if he was dead,' he says, producing his dick, which is pierced with an exceptionally heavy Prince Albert. He starts to urinate over the body as Alice and Sasha shout at him. Sasha looks at me, as if I could do anything about this.

'As his master pissed all over him he lay motionless pretending to be dead, like the great useless fat lump he always was.'

Richard zips himself up, underlining each word with a kick in the stomach.

'We do not have time for your childish games,' says Cathy, raising her voice slightly.

Richard looks over at her, still snarling. 'Oh, yes, and what do you propose to do about it?'

Cathy stands and walks over slowly to where Richard has moved into some sort of martial arts posture, legs slightly bent and wedged fingers extended in front of him. He has one of his frightening faces on as he dances around on the tips of his toes.

'I do not believe you have a black belt,' she says. But she has to look up to say this as he is about eight inches taller than her.

'Prove it, then,' he says.

'You must prove your ability to me,' she says. She is standing legs slightly apart, hands crossed in front of her chest. She looks very relaxed indeed.

'I only hit women when they ask me to, dear.'

'I'm asking you to.'

'You don't know what you're talking about, you daft tart.'

'I have trained in aikido, karate and judo. I was three times junior champion of Hong Kong in kendo, and I see my sensei regularly for private tuition in . . .'

Richard launches a fast-flying kick, which probably would have broken her pelvis if she had still been standing where Richard had aimed himself. As soon as he lands she is on him from behind, in a blur of arms and legs, bringing him to the floor by kicking the back of both knees. She even lets him struggle to his feet, and it can only be whatever drugs he has taken that persuade him to go on to certain defeat at her hands. Not to mention those shiny purple boots. He is potentially stronger, of course, but she is never where he expects her to be and, after a kick in the nuts has him curled up in the foetal position, she straddles him and starts to throttle him. Apart from a faint sheen of sweat on her forehead she still looks unruffled as she starts to employ some highly erotic strangulation techniques of her own.

Richard isn't getting much from this – except the chance to submit for a change, to see how the other half lives – but the rest of us get to see her short skirt ride up over her thighs as she blocks off Richard's windpipe. She is wearing very white, very brief knickers – since you ask – and the throttling process requires her to thrust her muscular rump in the air as she presses her body weight down on to his neck. Perhaps a chokehold doesn't strictly require such a display of gleaming thigh and tight knickers, but it would seem that the goddess Venus has been listening to the fervent prayers of Sasha and I.

The comedic muses must be listening too, as Richard flails his arms and legs about without connecting with anything. Sasha started applauding somewhere around the time that Richard hit the deck for the second time, and now she is doing some absurd

American cheerleader's dance. I could stand a fair amount of
Sasha waving imaginary pompons around and, more important,
looking happy for the first time in ages, but then she spoils it by
going into her sparring routine once Cathy has loosened her
chokehold and is stood smoothing down her skirt. Watching
Sasha ducking and weaving, throwing the odd punch while
smiling beatifically, is impossibly cute until I remember that it
used to belong to me. I thought that was our little game. Sasha
stops as soon as she sees Cathy is not amused and then sits down
as soon as Cathy does. We would appear to have a new leader.
Which is fine by me. It appears that I was grovelling to the right
person all along.

'Well, then,' says Sasha, after we have all told Cathy how
wonderful she is – all of us except Richard, that is; he's not
saying anything right now. Even Alice seems to nod her approval,
but it's hard to tell through the smoke.

'Where are we going to bury Hugh?' says Sasha, to me.

'What do you want to bury me for?' I say.

'That's not funny, Matt.'

It's still annoying her, though. Which is why I'm still saying it.

Richard groans as he crawls over to where his cigarettes are,
one hand clutched around his throat. Alice helps him to sit up
and lights one for him and one for herself. It almost brings a
lump to the throat watching her doing something as selfless as
that.

'We could tell the police he is a tragic accident,' says Cathy.

Sasha smiles fondly at this little grammatical glitch.

'He was a tragic accident the day he was born,' she says as
Richard, a ghost of his former self, starts to cough hard enough
to expel sputum. It's too loud to ignore, especially when Alice
joins in too.

'The dawn chorus,' says Sasha, genuinely disgusted for once.

'You are wasting time. We must make a decision,' says Cathy firmly. 'We could take him in the cab?' she says to me.

'Why not Richard's car?'

'Didn't bring it, dear boy,' he croaks. 'So you will actually be of some use for once. Come on, let's get him dressed.'

But first Richard goes over to where Stanley's body is taking up far too much space. You would have to have a heart of stone not to be moved by Richard gently easing the body of his dead dog into a binbag, but I manage it somehow.

'You know, I think he wanted to die and this way he could ruin all of our lives,' announces Sasha. She is standing there like she is expecting a round of applause or something.

'He willed his own heart attack?' I say, wrapping strong thick tape around Hugh's body, which Cathy is holding bent double.

Richard shrugs. 'I could turn my body off if I wanted to.'

'Why don't you, then? Do us all a favour,' says Sasha.

Richard picks up the noose.

'Aaah. To think he'll never get to play with this again. Brings a tear to your eye. Anyone have any objection to keeping Hugh at my place?'

There are some shrugs and blank faces. No one knows what to say to a man who insists on taking home a corpse to play with.

'What are we waiting for, then?' says Richard, rubbing his hands together.

'For you to shut up, as usual,' says Sasha. She picks up the gun and points it at him.

Richard just puts his tongue out at her. 'You don't even know if that has any bullets in it,' he says.

She lets off a shot at his feet, which has him leaping in the air. I wait for Cathy to give her a severe chiding, which I was expecting from our skipper, but instead there is only the soft, sweet sound of her laughter.

'Let's get out of here,' says Sasha, now restored to Supreme Ogress status once more.

I'm certainly not planning on leading the mutiny against these two any time soon so I work hard on folding Hugh's putrid bulk in two, then taping it together. There is a brief nervy interlude until we find a packing case to fit him in, and then Richard and I carry him down the stairs.

10

'THIS IS THE fog I came to London for!' Cathy says. 'Sherlock Holmes! *The Hound of the Baskervilles!*'

Sasha has heard me, at length, on the subject of tourists who expect London to be fogbound, but once I've seen the innocent joy on Cathy's face I shelve all that.

'Matt hates Sherlock Holmes,' says Sasha, eyes shining and teeth agleam as she waits to see how I will cope. This isn't at all true, but I pretend I care more about getting us to Hampstead in one piece than what Cathy thinks as we cross Battersea Bridge to where the parasites live.

Soon the road is clogged up with professional heirs and heiresses; too many stripy shirts, unnecessary sunglasses and shiny sports cars. Now I have Hugh's gun in my leather jacket I am in a position to live out my fantasies, but the real targets are sitting in the back of our cab. My supposed allies just *love* Chelsea, of course.

'Look at that darling little pub,' enthuses Sasha. Cathy actually bounces up and down on her seat as she points out a bright red telephone kiosk and the hanging baskets of flowers. She can probably close her eyes and see a bowler-hatted Steed and Emma Peel pulling up outside in their Bentley.

'It's Irish now,' I say. 'Gaelic football, horse racing and teeth and bone fragments in your beer once they all get going.'

'You have to get rid of this cab,' says Sasha, and there is genuine disgust in her voice.

'Every time you drive this thing you become a Nazi. It's spirit possession, it really is.'

'What's unusual is that it's also full of young women,' I say, trying to regain ground.

'You're saying women don't drink?' says Sasha. As if I could forget her tequila and table-dancing antics.

'Not usually in pubs,' I say wearily.

'Not in your day, Granddad.'

I let it pass. I need to be fresh for the next argument. Shouldn't have too long to wait now. Richard opens his mouth and not too long afterwards there is a scuffle, but I have switched my walkman on by then. They settle down again once Cathy has flicked the underside of Richard's nose with a fingernail. I have the feeling he is going to extract a terrible revenge for these humiliations sometime soon, but right now he is preoccupied with cradling the binbag containing the mortal remains of Stanley the Rhodesian Ridgeback. He even has a tear in his eye at one point, but I somehow restrain myself from suggesting a group hug.

As we eventually approach the summit of Richard's quiet leafy street, I can tell Sasha is jealous of the big detached house that is high enough up to enable him to sneer at the entire city over his breakfast spliff. He has let the garden decay, though, and opening the front door lets us into an ambience in which Hugh is going to feel right at home. The ground floor smells of rubber, dog, disinfectant and skunk. The pedal bin is overflowing, as is every surface and shelf. Richard's distinctive artwork is everywhere, mostly large drawings of his dog sporting an unfeasibly large erection. He often sneers at the concept of love, but he seems to have felt something for that dog. He lays the black binbag containing his remains very carefully on one of the few uncluttered bits of floor.

'You going to bury him in the garden?' I say. I try to look sympathetic, although he has done little to earn it. Needless to say, it comes right back in my face.

'I'm going to have him stuffed,' he says. Then his wrinkly skin stretches tight over his bony face and his teeth come out to announce yet another forced grin. 'Why change the habits of a lifetime?'

I look round for my little terrier, but she is busy laughing too loudly at something Cathy has said. Relieved that she didn't hear this, I clear some takeaway cartons off the couch and sit down. From where I sit I can see four overflowing ashtrays. Alice drifts over to one of these, although it makes little difference whether the ash goes in there or on to the floor with everything else.

Spread around the bare floorboards are some scrofulous old mattresses and an old maroon settee that may be exuding the all-pervading air of stale decrepitude that goes with the broken lightbulb hanging from the ceiling and the black and green stuff growing out of a silver takeaway carton.

'Is that a Joseph Beuys?' I say to Sasha, pointing out a particularly lurid fungoid splodge with hairs growing out of it, obviously a work still in progress. I am hoping to rekindle a long-forgotten feud that was originally triggered by the news that a German cleaning woman had inadvertently wiped a Beuys *meisterwerk* off a gallery wall. The work in question had been a random accumulation of dirt and grease; there may have been cobwebs involved – as usual, I can't remember – but I thought the woman who wiped it up had a valid point. Sasha nearly left me that afternoon, but right now she just narrows her eyes a little and shakes her head. It's nice to see her mellowing. Another thirty years of this and I might be allowed to put one of my Bernard Manning videos on again.

'What are we going to do about the money?' says Sasha. 'He owed me a couple of grand from last week.'

'You wouldn't work without cash upfront,' says Richard.

Sasha reaches into her hard knobbly rubber shoulder bag and produces a small folder, inside which is an IOU written in blood. I want to tell her that this is potential evidence for the prosecution, but I also want to see her wipe the floor with Richard.

'It's my money,' says Sasha. 'That's his writing. That's his blood.'

Even Alice's jaw drops at that one. 'That's illegal,' she says, studying the spidery handwriting.

'It was legally binding as far as we were concerned.'

'Yes, dear, I'm sure you spent a lot of time binding him to various things, but why shouldn't we share this little windfall?' says Richard. 'After all, with Matt's money, why do you need to be a dominatrix anyway?'

He turns to me, and either I can lay my life down in a futile attempt at wiping that smile off his face or I can make myself even more bitter, sick and twisted by staying silent. Which is what I do.

'We really have more important concerns,' says Cathy.

It's interesting to watch Sasha bottling it up rather than arguing with Cathy, but Richard's frown and index finger held aloft seem to mean that an important statement is on its way.

'We must be very careful,' he says. 'There is every chance that he will pick one of our bodies to reincarnate in.' He nods gravely at Sasha, who is taking this far too seriously for my liking.

'Indeed, there is not a moment to lose,' I say.

Four of them turn to look at me, there is a moment's silence then they all turn away again, which hurts much more than any cutting remarks. Soon they are all talking at once, as usual, but Richard inevitably wins out. 'Most cultures believe in reincarnation,' he is saying. 'The British did until it was wiped out by that nonsense called Xtianity. The Vikings used to take great care at funerals, approaching the corpse backwards with a hand over their anuses to prevent any stray spirits from entering them.'

'Rather like visitors to your house, Richard,' says Sasha.

Richard just shows her some gleaming white teeth then vanishes for the moment. It's hard not to look at the bag where Hugh is currently enjoying his final confinement scenario.

'Well, he'll never get out of that one,' I say, but Sasha and Cathy are too busy with each other.

Just then we are all distracted by the sound of a screaming engine that seems to be driving some hideous metallic contraption. Richard appears hefting a chainsaw, the grinding metallic teeth just about drowning out his mechanical cackling.

He has no trouble, clearing a path over to the binbag or in lopping one of Hugh's fat flabby arms off before Sasha scurries off and switches the power off at the plug.

I just have time to check the arm out, and the glossy, red wiring spilling out of the socket, before I have to see what Richard is going to do next. While I'm staring at him I sense that Cathy is still staring at the glistening sinewy mess. I can't imagine why she should be so fascinated, but that is nothing new. I probably haven't a clue what Sasha or anyone else might be thinking either, although it is safe to say that Sasha is annoyed presently.

'Give me the gun,' she says, holding her hand out.

I should tell her not to be silly or go and have a nice cup of tea or something, but instead I give her the gun and she trains it on Richard. She has the two-handed stance down and the cold-eyed stare, and as it's only an hour or so since the last time she fired it you would think that Richard should look afraid.

'Still loaded?' he says, trying out a grin that slides off his face pretty quickly when she releases the safety catch.

'Try me,' she says.

They stare each other out until he looks away first, after which he gets his smoking tackle out and starts to skin up. Sasha gives me the gun back, which gives me the opportunity to check that there are in fact two bullets left. I had thought that nobody noticed the way my hands shook until I see Alice's poisonous little smirk.

Everyone else is looking at Richard's new piece of sculpture, in particular the arm socket, which looks a little like a plate of cold chicken cacciatora. The arm has been picked up by Cathy, who demurely asks where the bathroom is before waving it at us as she exits.

'Bye-ee!' she says, and then clumps up the stairs. I look at her hard rubber shoulder bag under the seat and wonder what's in it while Alice says, 'I didn't know she had a sense of humour.'

'Heart-warming, isn't it?' says Richard, sucking in pungent skunk smoke. We all have some of that, and then I go withdrawn and paranoid and Richard grins all the more. Alice is cross because she wants to use the bathroom. There is only one in the entire house.

'What's she doing in there?' she says. I've no idea of how long

Cathy has been gone now or of anything else except that I want to be home under a warm duvet, sucking my thumb.

'I'd better go and see whether she's locked herself in the lavvy,' says Richard, managing to imbue that statement with a casual misogyny that makes Sasha's jaw jut out in a dangerous fashion. Some time later Richard appears without his grin and, for the first time I can ever recall, looking frightened.

'She's gone. She must have climbed down the back way. With the arm.'

Sasha looks at me for an answer. As if I have any idea on this or anything else. 'Maybe she felt peckish,' I say.

Richard remembers that he has to be more transgressive than everyone else. 'And I so wanted to have him stuffed,' says Richard. 'He's ruined. Ruined!' He lifts Hugh up and perches him on his knee like a one-armed ventriloquist's dummy. 'All the king's horses and all the king's men couldn't put Humpty together again.'

'You're sick,' is about all I can manage, but it's two words too many.

Richard's laughter continues to sound inside and outside my head. If he ever stops, which doesn't seem likely, I'll still be able to hear it loud and clear. I put my head in my hands and stare at the floor for a while. When I look up again they are all still there, Hugh is still dead and we are still implicated in what some busybodies will probably see as murder.

'We have to get out of here,' says Richard. 'I have a houseboat that no one knows about. In Greenwich. If we take the cab it's perfect cover. Fancy going south of the river, guv?'

I hate to admit it, but he's right. The police are never going to stop a taxi.

It takes a long time for everyone to get organised, during

which I slip Cathy's bag inside my leather jacket. That means we have the only clue as to her whereabouts.

It's not much, but it lightens the gloom slightly as we begin the long, slow journey south.

WE DROP OFF RICHARD, Alice and the mortal remains of Hugh in Greenwich and then head for home, Sasha taking a catnap curled up on the back seat. After struggling through the usual heavy traffic and oppressive boredom that goes with any London Sunday, I just want to worship the sun that never fails to light my world – a Bang & Olufsen widescreen television with an indestructible silver remote control. Needless to say, Sasha isn't standing for this and insists on a hot bath scented with some herbs which will cleanse our auras of any toxic residue left over from Hugh's death. I can usually go along with this sort of thing, as even white magic usually requires flesh communion at some point but, just as the candlelight and the massage are starting to work she whispers something terrifying in my ear.

'I'm fertile right now.'

'Great.'

'Come on, you said you wanted children.'

After some preliminary whining I say, 'I don't know. Having

sex while trying to have a child still feels a bit . . . I don't know, kinky. If not downright dangerous.'

'At least we are both alive.'

The significance of that eludes me until I remember Richard's occasional teasing references to necrophilia.

'Who do you think he will try first?' I ask. 'Hugh or the dog?'

She winces, on the dog's behalf, of course. I don't waste too much time wondering where Richard might be stuffing his beringed and weighted magic wand; it's usually somewhere most people think it shouldn't be. There are so many other things to worry about: the disappearance of Cathy with what may eventually be evidence in a murder trial, a possible transfer to the big league in America and a slow painful death after fifteen years on death row, if anyone ever connects the string of corpses we left behind us last Easter. And we still don't know who nailed a skinned cat to our door, or what Richard and Alice might do with Hugh's corpse left to their own devices.

After all this and more has been discussed at length, and the theatre of hostilities has moved from the bathroom to the living-room, Sasha arranges her limbs in the lotus position and closes her eyes.

I suppose a cheap pornographer would mention her shaven mound at this point, with its lightning-flash brand just above the stark divide of the cleft. Well, as it is rather eye-catching, and tactile also, we might as well mention it. And once that has been duly noted, it seems appropriate to focus on the contrasting scents of her body, the eager look in her eye and the sound of her impassioned sigh – all of which bring to mind certain aspects of our shared history. I manage to concentrate on that and somehow ignore the dread possibilities of conception for long enough to reach the eager anticipation Sasha was trying for half an hour ago.

The sex soon splits into its usual physical manifestation and the more rigorous cerebral arena where endless comparisons are made between all the things it's ever been; what it might be, what it should be, what people say it is in print, what Sasha says it is and my ideas about what she may be thinking, what my memories are (real and speculative), the ever-expanding library of images and ideas I have accessed from the net and videos and . . . some other made-up stuff. Some people call this union, and for some of the time it actually is. As for those helpless romantics who still use sex as a bonding ritual with their partner, what is the point when Sasha is probably thinking about Cathy anyway? I'm certainly not taking the risk of serenading her mentally when she is probably up on the roof caterwauling with Cathy.

We drift on anyway, sometimes together, sometimes apart. There are false starts, startling revelations, bits that seem like hard work, bits that used to work and have lost their lustre, very good bits indeed, and perennial favourites that never fail. As usual, both parties to the original agreement reserve the right to redefine all of the above categories at any time, but at some stage there will be the point where the yang essence finally comes to the boil. Rather than spill this, I usually hoard it by a simple orgasm-enhancing clenching process that most Western males remain blissfully ignorant of. It is here that any halfway competent magus is supposed to send out healing vibrations or deadly curses but, perhaps distracted by the possibility of a single sperm leaking past the barrier of muscle, the image that flashes through my head during orgasm is Richard's Cheshire cat grin and Hugh's corpse.

After some disturbed twitchy sleep, Sasha puts on a video of some gritty cop drama, part of our landlord John's Helen Mirren collection. I'm too weak to protest, so soon we are cast adrift on the streets of Manchester with the sort of street drug dealer they have on television, a charismatic Machiavellian figure who is perfectly in control of his destiny. The street ones we know tend to have skin like tofu and no remaining brain cells, but this guy is different.

'Who's that?' says Sasha, coming back from the kitchen with more Orange Dazzler herbal tea.

'Guy calls himself "The Street". Because he controls the street.'

Sasha sighs and picks up a book of photographs of small injured Japanese women in splints, slings and plaster casts. Like her own earlier work, some think this stuff is art with a capital A; some regard it as evidence for the prosecution.

'I want to be "The Couch",' I say, probably to myself. 'Because I rule the couch.'

'Says who?'

'You're going to have to fight me for it.'

All of a sudden she casts the book aside and is on her feet, dancing around while throwing the occasional punch my way. It looks as lovely as it ever did, but since she did it in Cathy's presence the other day yet more of our shared past has been irreparably tarnished. It's by no means certain that Sasha's craze for Cathy is the usual three-day flu that can be cured by bedrest and overdosing on the infectious virus. It's long been part of our contract that we can sleep with other people, but the way things look there may soon be a new contract, one between Sasha and Cathy. And my next contract will be between me and my trusty right hand. All things considered, I would still rather build on what Sasha and I have already created. It might be fiction, but it seems real to us. I certainly don't want to be written out before we have barely started. But even sex has to take second place to whoever is nailing cats to our door.

'Hugh could have been the Dungeonmaster's Apprentice,' I say.

'I was not the Dungeonmaster's Apprentice,' she replies. 'See! It's not funny! It's not!'

'If you say so, dear.'

The room quakes as she hovers on the edge of a major seethe, but luckily she just kills the television, settles back on the couch and closes her eyes. Soon she is muttering something deep, slow and resonant, which is probably an invocation of some ancient female deity.

'Yes!' she says, sitting bolt upright.

I slump further down into the couch knowing what this could mean. It would appear that she has channelled some important information.

'The bald figure on the roof could have been a woman,' she says.

'The man who nailed the cat to our door was a woman?' I say, as neutrally as I can.

'Why not?'

'He seemed to be running like a man. And I'm pretty sure he had a wispy goatee.'

'So do women who take male hormones,' grits Sasha, perhaps trying to imply that this is common knowledge. 'This would give them the option of living both as a man and as a woman.'

'Or it could be a hermaphrodite,' I say, not entirely seriously.

'Yes! Remember Jenny.'

I had managed to forget Jenny. A man/woman in his/her fifties who looked like Alastair Sim in drag. He actually was a genuine hermaphrodite, although no one ever wanted to get close enough to find out exactly what this entailed.

'If it was Jenny, at least we could tell him, or her, to go and fuck himself.'

'Yeah, yeah. What if it was a threat to the guy whose flat this is?'

'John? All he ever does is smoke dope and play the piano. He's far too innocent to attract this, and in any case why would whoever it is include photos of us? He's been touring Brazil for months. Look, as you well know as a sex worker, death threats come with the territory. Nothing will happen.'

I don't believe this, and it's clear from Sasha's sceptical expression that neither does she.

Only maniacs skin cats and nail them to the door, and the crucifix could be a clear reference to Sasha's earlier blasphemous art or the so-called black magic we have long been involved with.

We are clearly in mortal danger, but that doesn't stop Sasha from adding to the grief quotient by putting on a CD of some moth-eaten old free jazz, congas and randomly approximate trumpet and some chanting that must have meant something at the time. Someone who shouldn't have bothered attempts a bowed double-bass solo to the accompaniment of insistent percussion. It's exactly the right sound for a discussion about the nailing of a skinned cat to our door.

'Who else have we offended recently?' I say, as the dirge continues.

'Maybe not even recently. When you were drinking. All those satanic death threats you used to send.'

It's embarrassing to remember what I used to do, another cross alcoholics have to bear. When Sasha's smile has squeezed all the juice out of that one, she says: 'Whoever it was could now be wearing a wig to disguise themselves. And you know there are those tattoos that fade after a month or so. That Indian skin dye.'

'Yes,' I say testily, getting irritated by Sasha's deductive zeal as I generally do. 'So, to sum up,' I say. 'We are looking for man, or a woman, or a hermaphrodite. Who is bald but may well be wearing a wig. A number of tattoos were visible but these may, of course, be removable or fade in time.'

'All right! You don't have to be so nasty about it. I'm just thinking out loud.' She leaves a pause long enough for me to start feeling guilty.

'Why don't you do what the police do, just get hold of someone who will fit and hang it on them?' I say.

'Well, at least we won't have to hang Hugh any more, and don't you dare . . .'

'Wouldn't dream of it.'

'The police usually wait for someone to tell them who did it.'

'What is it with you and Alice anyway?' she says. 'Did you fuck her?'

'I can honestly say I have never fucked her.'

She's still waiting.

'Look, it's nothing earth-shattering.'

'Why would she keep a secret anyway? She hates you.'

'Because, obviously, I know something about her. Look, it's nothing you need to know. In any case the only reason you want to solve this so-called mystery is that your childhood was so fucked up. You'll never find an answer to that, and you'll never find an answer to this.'

'I hate you. I absolutely hate you.'

All of a sudden I can't stand the random brass braying that is getting on my tits for the last ten minutes. 'What on earth *is* that?' I say.

'It's Don Cherry.'

I sigh, remembering that I spent some of my youth pretending to like this stuff. Now it sounds like what it actually is, a man with almost no technique blundering about in the dark. For no reason at all he plays a great quavering swoop more or less up and down an octave, although with lots of snags where he seems to have caught his dick in his zip. Some trumpet players can be bombastic and flashy, not something you could say about Don. After more than two decades of handsomely remunerated journalism suggesting that anyone who knows anything about music should be prevented from making any ever again, there is probably no point saying any of this, but I'm just too weak presently to suffer in silence. The next trumpet mewl makes me groan out loud, which is enough to set Sasha off.

'When did you become this fascist control freak who has to allow one type of sound to be heard?' she says.

'He can't fucking play. That's it.'

Another ham-fisted flurry ends with a genuine Bronx cheer.

'That could, without exaggeration, have been produced by shoving the instrument up his arse and . . .'

'You *are* a fascist! You're a dinosaur!'

'I was pretending to like John Cage by the time you were six,' I say. This is true, but it doesn't have the effect I had imagined during rehearsal. Now I've ruined that track for her, Sasha puts MTV on for revenge and is soon bobbing her head while four scowling black teenagers in improbable hats circle a camera at floor level, taking it in turns to kick at the lens. They are shouting about something or other while twisting their fingers into silly shapes. Sasha likes it, though, nodding sagely at each macho boast. She wouldn't take this crap from white boys so I have to say something. 'Neo-Nazis wouldn't be allowed airtime to portray blacks like that . . .'

'Like it's better having Wynton Marsalis playing prehistoric jazz in a sports jacket. And talking about how much he loves his mummy and daddy.'

She pretends to throw up then goes back to bobbing her head.

It *is* catchy. Even my foot is tapping as I bitch on. 'And as a feminist? All that stuff about ho's and bitches?'

'You just hate them having all that money. And being young.'

'Yeah, I really miss having nowhere to live and hangovers and drunken fistfights and mad women . . .'

'I'm not mad . . .'

' . . . and duffle coats and long greasy hair and experimenting with beards and thinking that Woody Allen was sophisticated and John Fowles was infinitely wise.'

It's painfully embarrassing saying that out loud, but luckily it's a long time since Sasha wanted to hear about my past so it floats past her. It's probably time to feed her another line about the skinned cat anyway.

'Maybe Cathy arranged all this,' I say. 'It seems suspicious that Cathy showed up just when the hate mail started.'

She shrugs. We may never know. Unless we find Cathy again.

'What was in her bag?' she says. Much less money than the first time I looked, but I just look blank and go and get the bag from the hall.

'I'm sure it contains a valuable clue,' I say, exasperated by her insistence that it is possible to link up the past, present and future in any meaningful way. I upend the bag on the floor, trying to ignore the thought that this feels more intrusive than carting Hugh's remains about. In among the many cosmetic items is a wallet with a blood donor's card, the fancy black Torture Garden membership card with the gold tethered woman emblazoned on it, and a AA twelve-step card which is considerably less impressive – just a little bit of white card folded into two. There is also a pocket guide to London meetings which has turned grey and smudgy with repeated use. This guide gives you starting times and a list of dank, depressing church halls to go to. It doesn't tell you where you can find a meeting which isn't full of grim, chain-smoking Celts, though, because they all are. I have to stifle a snicker at the thought of Sasha intruding on one of these grim gatherings of the undead but, on second thoughts, she wouldn't have to act the addict stuff, and she certainly likes baring her soul in front of strangers. Group-encounter therapy holds few terrors once you have stood naked on a stage opening yourself up with a speculum and shining a torchlight up the old Jade Gate.

'She's underlined a lot of meetings,' I say. 'Must have been one of those "a hundred meetings in a hundred days" junkies.'

'You're sure you won't get hooked on this stuff again?' says Sasha, looking rather concerned. 'I used to hate it when you would spout all that crap. I'd almost rather see you start drinking again.'

'Don't worry. I'm cured,' I say wearily.

Alcoholics Anonymous was surprisingly easy to kick, even though it was with their help that I managed to stop drinking in the first place. You can tire very quickly of other people's cigarette smoke, mad staring eyes, yet another prematurely aged Scottish or Irish man with a face like a fresh train-smash talking for ever, while the rest of the gang fidget on their rickety chairs waiting for him to shut up so they can embark on their ten minutes of glory.

'The biggest problem is that you aren't supposed to take drugs,' I say. 'While they sit there indulging in a non-stop stewed tea and cigarettes binge they wish to deny you the simple soporific pleasures of cannabis. And as we all know, acid can be thera-peutic.'

Which is bollocks. I know it and Sasha knows it. She groans and puts her head in her hands before bouncing back quickly.

'Any drug in small quantities can be beneficial,' she says. 'You are never going to take anything in small quantities. You are a hopeless addict. Try to accept it.'

She is wagging her finger at me, something you can like in certain circumstances, but I don't want to be lectured right now. I want cherishing. What I'm going to get is a rigorous analysis of my many deficiencies. Yet again I seem to have lost the remote control. There is no way of switching channels or even of turning her down a bit. And to make it worse, she's right. Again.

'There is no middle way,' she says. 'You have tasted the forbidden fruit. Either accept that you will be miserable without it or take it again. Either way, I don't want to hear any more about it. We have to find Cathy! Now!'

'Yes, we really must solve the mystery of the disappearing arm. It's not really to do with you wanting to shag her. You never had a freckled Eurasian before. That's what this is about. And why should I help you fall in love with someone else?'

There. I've said it now. It soon becomes apparent that this was not prudent. Five minutes into a long harangue which she is delivering while stomping around the room it is becoming clear that even turning the television off as a mark of respect will not be enough to save me this time.

'It has to be now!' shrieks Sasha, the climax of a long symphonic variation on the theme that I don't care. Enough. About something or other. Unfortunately, like a lot of symphonies, Sasha's performance took too long to get going, and the result seemed hardly worth the time and trouble involved. Sasha's rants have all been done before anyway, and how can you recapture the initial excitement of knowing you're not going to be allowed to say anything for at least another ten minutes? While Sasha downloads the entire contents of her head, I sit there doing what I have been booked to do, which is to nod occasionally. At some point, not for any logical reason, she switches to the evils of the demon drink.

'It's drink that makes these things happen! It's a much bigger problem than drugs! It's drink – and drugs – that causes people to overstep their limits!' she says. I'm still nodding, somehow. 'He drank a lot. He should never have had that heart attack.'

'If that was what it was,' I say.

'You think it's murder?'

'Yes, I do.'

'Why?'

'I think someone knew that those masks are dangerous because you are breathing in what was in your lungs after a while.'

I watch her very carefully while I say this, and she looks surprised. But she's fooled me before. Not that it matters if she had decided to kill Hugh, but I wish she wouldn't lie to me. As he used to say himself in a different context, trust is a must, especially now that she's falling – fallen? – in love with Cathy. I don't want to end up as another convenient drug overdose like her first husband.

As the occasional sob blends into her frantic blather, I realise that I am somehow going to have to manoeuvre my bulk upright and out of the door to an AA meeting. And find Cathy. And find out who the Dungeonmaster's Apprentice is. And infiltrate Richard's gang, the Black Order – in case it's connected with the Dungeonmaster's Apprentice thing, but mostly because Sasha doesn't like to be excluded from anything.

'There's one in Soho, starts in an hour. She's underlined it,' says Sasha finally. Is this a pause? Too soon to say just yet but, yes, it probably is. But now there's nothing for me to say. Until I see her clothes in the context of an AA meeting.

'Do you think that . . .?'

Sasha can tell I'm afraid of completing the question so she

blitzes me with an interrogative eyebrow. I can't complete my question about her choice of dress without risking a knock-down, drag-out fight, but someone has to say something. I nod towards her fishnet stockings and rubber skirt and the black T-shirt on which is emblazoned a pair of fluorescent red lips. 'It's a bit much for the average street alkie,' I say. 'Most of them are Catholics. You might tip them over the edge.'

'It's probably because they are afraid of sexuality that they became alcoholics in the first place.'

'Yes, but you have to respect their space. It's all they have.'

Sasha is so surprised at this outburst of decency that she doesn't say anything until it's time to get in the cab and drive to Soho.

12

THE CHURCH HALL basement tucked away in 'London's Theatreland' is full, which is either good news for the recovery movement or just that this is the least worst thing to do on a Sunday afternoon, being cheaper than a movie and you get free tea and biscuits. After entering, people gravitate towards the all-important tea urn, behind which is a woman with a battered face and red flabby arms. She is wearing a floral dress that might have been appropriate in the countryside two or more decades ago and is serving a long line of sunburned street dossers with faces as creased and ugly as discarded crisp packets. I manage to get stewed tea, biscuits and two uncomfortable chairs sorted out while Sasha asks people if they know Cathy. Even if she looked sad and virtuous, like everyone else, this would be a major breach of etiquette. As it is, her dress and demeanour are causing heads to turn. The AA equivalent of a bouncer finally appears, a dour white-faced man with a Tony Curtis hairstyle and musty thrift-shop clothes. He may not have bought these

items in a thrift shop, but it's definitely time to send them
there.

'This meeting is really only for alcoholics,' he says, quietly but
firmly. 'It's not a social club.'

'I am an alcoholic,' she says, and the smile she is offering him
is almost warm and vibrant enough to colour in his grey shirt
and drab tweed jacket, even enough to make his mouth twitch
briefly. 'It's just that I haven't seen my friend Cathy. An Asian
girl. I'm afraid she's lapsed. She's not answering the phone.'

'Yes. I know who you mean,' he says.

Everyone is now looking at us.

'Where is she?'

'Time to start,' shouts a red-faced man, one of many who
seem in imminent danger of coronary arrest.

'The chair is ready,' we are told, firmly. 'We'll talk later.'

I was expecting the sort of non-consensual torture that even
Sasha couldn't enjoy, and the first speaker doesn't disappoint me.
He has a horror story for us but, like Kenneth Branagh's Mary
Shelley's *Frankenstein*, the wrong person is the star and the effect
is ruined. We just don't care what happens to this guy. The next
speaker deconstructs the story of her life, playing with narrative
the way a cat might mangle a ball of wool. She doesn't know
how she got here, where she is now or where to go from here.
And now neither do we.

Someone throws a handful of slogans at her, then more glum
strangers meander through a heavily censored version of their
depravity. This lot wouldn't be much good at the Porno Olympics
because, as far as I can work out from listening to them, sex
doesn't actually exist. Jesus Christ keeps cropping up, though,
both in their stories and under my breath as the evening wears
on. By now the audience has imbibed so much caffeine and
nicotine that they are practically rattling in their seats, nerves all

ajangle, desperate for everyone else to shut the fuck up so they can say their piece.

After forty-five minutes I contemplate reopening my scarifications, not for any ritual or fetish purpose but just because I know it will hurt less than listening to this stuff. Not that any of the older hands are bothered – those who have won promotion from handing out the biscuits or stewing the tea to elder statesmen. They smell of hand-rolled tobacco and old-fashioned hair oil. Some of these men still sport the teddy boy quiffs of their youth, except the hair is grey and their rheumy eyes are walled in by cracks, wrinkles and deep fissures. Scars are an optional extra, and here I fit in with the crowd, but my skin is too soft, my clothes are too colourful. It is obvious I have not soiled my hands with manual work or recently done an honest day's work for a honest day's pay. If ever.

We sit there, heads bowed for a while, listening through a long speech by a man who has been sober for ten years. His air of brooding intensity is so dark and forbidding that I doubt if he has smiled in that time. 'For Christ's sake, lighten up and have a drink, mate,' would seem to be the only response to much of this stuff, but at least it gives me time to fantasise about setting up a rival self-help group, Coffeeaholics Anonymous, where we could all sit round getting drunk talking about how much coffee we used to drink. Almost frantic with boredom, I flick through one of their ancient leaflets, noting that it was written when spice-free stodge was the national diet, when alcoholics might have had difficulty 'keeping regular'.

I must be the only guy in the room who is praying that Sasha isn't going to say anything, but that soon becomes irrelevant as the door softly opens and Cathy arrives. As soon as she spots us I see surprise on her face for the first time, although it flares and dies in less than a second. I take longer to recover. I touch Sasha lightly on the arm as I stand to make my way up the aisle. Sasha's lips are compressed into a thin line and her eyes are dead, which lasts until Cathy gives us a rare, warm, gooey smile.

We might as well crawl the rest of the way. It's what we are going to be doing from now on anyway. We might as well get into practice.

'Hi Cathy,' says Sasha, rather cattily, probably trying to make her feel guilty but just showing how much she needs her.

Cathy waits till we are out on the street to reply, but then a limpet-like *Big Issue* salesman attaches himself to us. He gets very short shrift from Sasha, two short words delivered with the force of an upper cut which soon send him on his way. When he is far enough away not to get his ankles nipped he tells us we are 'out of order' and a lot of other stuff designed to make us feel guilty, but we are too busy looking at Cathy to burst into tears.

'Look, I just couldn't take any more of Richard this afternoon,' says Cathy. 'I suppose you found my bag. Have you still got it?'

'Yes. Have you still got the arm?' I say. The AA doorman or gloom-master or whatever they call him has come outside to check she is all right, but Cathy smiles and waves him on his way.

'Of course I've got the arm,' says Cathy. 'I'm going to tattoo it.' Which even shuts Sasha up. 'It's part of a long-term art project I'm interested in. I couldn't believe my luck when Richard sliced it off. Come to my place? For a coffee? It's just around the corner.'

'We thought you'd go to the police,' says Sasha, when she has recovered enough to speak.

A frown almost ripples across the calm surface of Cathy's face, but her voice is neutral as she says: 'Wait. Not here.'

We pass Bar Italia, where a crowd of middle-aged bankers

have gathered on gleaming bikes to masquerade as Hell's Angels, then turn into a badly lit alleyway where Cathy starts to fumble for her keys.

Two of the door bells advertise the sort of fiftyish sex workers who describe themselves as models, but Cathy's bell states simply TOP FLAT, which seems appropriate. She is certainly dominant enough be described as a top, in the argot of American perves, and she is still young enough to use the word the way the chemical generation do, to describe just about everything except having no drugs.

Her flat is furnished in the sort of minimalist style that never worked whenever Sasha and I attempted it. We once had everything silver and black, without any proper shelves or storage units, and tall, thin, rickety barstools instead of a big sofa. It just doesn't go with human habitation. Cathy Cheung, who is obviously not really human, has a clean flat and no clutter. There is something to covet everywhere you look. I eye the chrome cappuccino-maker and wonder what she does for money, as this is about four hundred quids' worth of kit.

Once Sasha has dived into the bathroom it seems like a good time to find out what Cathy wants with a severed arm. We both speak at the same time then smile politely, which stretches into an uneasy silence. There is a very long pause while I try to think of something worthy of her and also of the person I would like to be in her presence. Some helpful sprite tells me to relax and be myself, which probably means that I should guzzle a few high-octane German beers then switch to supermarket whisky while I ring up a few drug dealers. Then I should start swearing, shouting and singing, eventually dancing on the table. After being helped from the premises there would then be a long journey on automatic pilot. Bruises, dried blood and loose teeth would be the only clues as to whether I had been on the wrong side of a street brawl or had merely fallen down some stairs. There would occasionally be the cheery call of a constable alerting me to the fact that it is dawn and I have slept in a cell. Tempting as that scenario still is, I force the false, sober version of me to speak.

'What's the big deal about the arm?' I ask.

She looks at me for a long time and then says: 'I have always wanted a limb with which I could create something to satisfy me and me alone. Sometimes I tire of the stupid requests people make of me. The names of football teams or lovers. Sometimes I yearn for a canvas where I can let my imagination run wild.'

You can write all over me, darlin', breathes some lecherous baboon in my inner ear, but I ignore that and think of the many tattooists I have known who resolutely ignore what the customer wants and get on with bringing their own dreams alive. What she is saying makes some sort of twisted sense in this light, but this isn't the sort of behaviour you want from your fellow conspirators. She has already looked at me long enough to ensure that I won't be raising that particular point, though.

'Can you do my tattoo now?' I say.

'The runes? We made up a design, right?' She thinks for a while and say: 'Normally I wouldn't, but it will calm me down. I need to do something.'

She goes to get her stuff, all the while giving me a rehearsed speech about sterile conditions and aftercare tips. This is all good stuff coming from someone who has just stolen a dead man's arm, but I manage to keep a straight face until she's finished. Soon my arm has been shaven and swabbed, the runic design has been sketched on a transparency, and her tattoo gun is revved up and ready to go. It's so absorbing to watch even Sasha doesn't say anything.

'You ready?' says Cathy, a slight twitch at the corner of her mouth. For a brief moment I see her the way Sasha must see her, as they play their games, but then it's back to me sitting in the dentist's chair. And with tattooing, there is never any local anaesthetic, just whatever you can cook up yourself. I had actually been looking forward to an invigorating blast of pain until the opening incision changes my mind. But I'm here now. Might as well go through with it. If you didn't want this to be happening it would probably be quite painful, but it's just a matter of stepping into the pain, letting it flow through you. And gritting your teeth and trying not to whimper. Especially now Sasha has returned.

'Where are you from?' I say, trying to take my mind off the fierce, insistent pain.

'Hong Kong,' says Cathy, as the motor revs up and slows down. Our eyes meet as my blood flows slowly upwards.

'I know Hong Kong,' I say, before realising that Cathy couldn't care less and also that my smile is too wide – too wide for Sasha, although Cathy seems able to cope. 'What made you want to be a tattooist?' I say, which gets me a slight frown.

She rattles through the next bit quickly enough. She must have rehearsed it many times. 'My father was a tattooist, but it is dishonourable for a woman to learn tattooing. I picked up as much as I could from him and also practised on my friends.'

'I didn't know Chinese people liked tattoos,' said Sasha. 'Isn't it a Triad thing?'

'We had lots of European friends. I wanted to be modern. Not some little adoring Chinese wife.'

'You didn't want to be a gangster's moll.'

'What is a moll?'

'A floosie. A dame, a broad. A girlfriend,' says Sasha happily. 'Don't worry – he always talks like that. Words that have gone out of fashion. Like him.'

Cathy is too busy with her drill to reply.

'Did you ever do Hugh?' I say.

Cathy's voice clouds over and her voice sounds colder and harder as she replies. 'Hugh asked me to tattoo his dick. You know, the end part?'

'The glans, the bell end?' I say. There must be a better way of saying that, but Cathy's face has lit up.

As I bask in its radiance she opens her mouth to speak. 'Bell end,' she says. 'I like the sound of that.'

I'm smiling too hard again.

'Ding-dong,' says Sasha, sounding like a cracked bell.

I try staring her out but it's not going to work. Nothing is ever going to work ever again. I am in the dock at the Old Bailey and the black cap is on. The 'abuse excuse' isn't going to work and neither is 'guilty but insane'. It's time to dance the Tyburn Tarantella, and the only partner you need now is the guy in the black hood.

Time to change the subject. I remember that she did not ask the way to the bathroom but found it instantly, even though it is one of several matt-black doors.

'Anyone would think you had been here before,' I say.

'I don't have to tell you where I've been.'

'And did you know about this arm fetish of hers?'

'No, but it's a legitimate form of expression. I always wanted to use body parts in my work.'

'Great. Let's mount an exhibition. With Richard's body and Alice's head. It's a shame we threw that skinned cat away really.'

'Never mind. There might be another one by the time we get home.'

We share a weak smile as we remember that we are supposedly on the same side.

'It is not an arm fetish!' says Cathy from nowhere, and I don't know why she is so angry either. 'I am an artist. I sculpt flesh. Living and dead.'

'Read him that Krafft-Ebing thing,' says Sasha.

Cathy gives her a sharp look then opens a silver file cabinet and retrieves a small black leather notebook.

'This was my entry for the Porno Olympics,' she says. 'It's my life in the style of a Krafft-Ebing case history. You must know his *Psychopathia Sexualis*.'

'It's on my bedside table,' I say.

'Ignore him,' says Sasha, as she so often does.

'It is also a homage to Terence Sellers who wrote her biography in this style,' says Cathy. 'I am going to read this and you are going to keep quiet.'

After checking that I am not pulling faces or fidgeting, she begins to read in her annoyingly calm voice: 'Father alcoholic, mother hysterical. The youngest of three sisters and subject to abuse from her father as a result of frustrating his desire for a male child. Subject fantasised frequently about whippings, mutilations, torture, violence, eventually trying to sublimate this passion for blood and violence into art only to find that this career was closed to a Chinese woman. Subject suffered from neurasthenia, which she treated with alcohol and various medicaments which did not suit her constitution. Returned to martial arts after becoming a recovering alcoholic. Dabbled briefly in the occult before deciding that this was another little boy's club she had no wish to be excluded from. Managed to channel obsession with sex and death into her artwork. As a tattooist she sculpts in live flesh and blood and has recently become obsessed with cadavers as a flesh canvas. Has indulged in consensual s/m long enough to realise that her deepest wishes and desires are outside the liberal consensus. Her dearest wish is to kill an unwilling subject by tattooing them slowly and painfully to death.'

She closes the book and stares directly at me. My immediate impulse is to call for a mini-cab or, even better, just dive out of the nearest window, but it soon becomes apparent she wants approval.

'Yeah,' I say. 'Very . . . powerful.'

'I love that stuff about tattooing someone to death,' says Sasha. 'I wish you would do it to Richard.'

'Or Alice,' I say.

'I want to get rid of Richard *and* Alice,' says Cathy.

She's talking very quietly, but she has our full attention.

'Getting rid of?' I say.

'Richard is clearly dangerous and unstable. Alice is also a random factor. They could both endanger our safety.'

'Getting rid of?' I say.

'Come on, Matt,' says Sasha. 'You've done it before. You can do it again.'

'Why me?' I say.

'Because you're so good at it, darling,' says Sasha, turning on the pout and the big misty eyes, the combination that used to really get to me. That was before I found out it could be manufactured to fit any occasion, from mortal danger to running out of decaffeinated coffee beans.

'When was the last time you said darling, darling?' I say, feeling a familiar rage eating me up again. 'Probably the last time you wanted something and . . .'

'If I could say something here,' says Cathy, and we both instantly shut up and turn our heads towards her. 'It seems most likely that someone in the occult community would have arranged for the skinned cat to be nailed to your door. Richard knows all of the people who are capable of such a thing. Assuming it isn't him. And anyway, doesn't Alice seem more likely? Especially after you had that fight.'

'A cat fight,' I say, and then turn to collect my fond smile from Sasha. But although she loves to compare herself to cats, and to various feline divinities, it seems I'm not allowed to. Not at the moment anyway, not while she is obsessed with a certain sleek glossy Siamese with very sharp claws. And Cathy draws patterns with her claws, then spits blood into the fresh wounds to make living, breathing pictures. What can I do to compete with that?

Luckily, Sasha can't see my hurt face because Cathy Is Speaking. As she is delivering a lecture on the use of tattooed body parts in contemporary art, I don't have to listen, giving me time to consider that maybe I should just wait for Cathy to stop becoming an unobtainable object of desire. Once they have feasted on each other long enough to know what might happen in advance, the spell will be broken. Nobody except the authors of romantic fiction and other liars can keep up that level of obsession for long; the only question is whether I have the patience to wait for the heat to die down. As it inevitably must. I can't really see them hand in hand down at Sainsbury's, arguing over rennet-free cheese or whatever miracle herbal tea Sasha has recently read about. Cathy could never take my place as the big grumpy teddy bear she needs to cuddle up to and occasionally kick round the room. And this service is even more indispensable now that her daddy shot himself in front of her last year. Or so I like to think anyway. But right now I can forget about all that because Cathy is stroking the enormous tattoo which covers my left arm.

'Who did this?'

'Andy. He's a real artist. He does what he wants to do, and the paying customer can get stuffed. Sometimes he's right, though. I wanted huge magic mushrooms, and he just put them inside the little S for Sasha.'

'That's cute. This is a tarot card?'

She actually stroked my upper arm when it was necessary only to glance down to where the hawk-headed magus in a purple robe stands before a table set with the tools of his trade, the whole thing set inside a black sun.

'It's a midnight version of the original.'

'I like big tattoos,' she says approvingly, patting my arm, which she really doesn't have to do at this point. 'Strong geometric shapes. So you can see them from across the room.' I have heard this before from tattooists, and it's not hard to see why they would prefer strong, bold designs to minimalism.

'That's because you get paid more,' I say.

I might just as well have slapped her. She takes a step back and seems to be deciding whether to use that tattoo drill on my face. She still doesn't look that animated, but her expression still cuts like a knife. And though I'm fond of certain types of savage stimulation, her flint face is causing me the sort of useless pain you get from stubbing your toe or jangling your elbow.

'I never do a tattoo I have no interest in just for the money,' she says.

I sit up straighter, resolving to be a better, purer, nobler person in future. 'Not even to learn, just to get technique?'

'That's how you divorced yourself from the magic of music,' said Sasha, wagging a finger at me.

'Thank you, dear,' I say, but she's right. I did it just for money so often I ended up cynical and jaded. That was part of the protective armour, of course, but eventually there was no heart left to preserve from the sound of terrible music. Just as recreational sex is unlikely to be the first thing on a middle-aged streetwalker's mind when she turns the meter off and heads for home, eventually even real music just sounds like more noise. It also reminds you how terrible the stuff you play for money is.

Silence is the stuff I treasure. Not that you can find any, of course.

'Shall we leave that off for the moment?' I say to Cathy now her tape of miserable students with guitars has finished.

'I like music. It helps me concentrate,' she says.

I nod grimly. It's always the hardest part of tattooing, putting up with the artist's choice of music. Once my fresh bleeding wound has had cream gently patted into it and been packed in polythene to stop it ruining my shirt, I walk around for a while to taste the excess energy that the tattoo has given me. With three runes wound around my wrist I am now sorted for the power of the sun, the mystic energies of the moon and the tricky shape-shifting abilities of Odin himself. Or Mercury, if you prefer your occult references untainted by the merest hint of Nazi misuse. Whether these runes will be enough against these two witches is another matter, of course.

Cathy and Sasha are now sat opposite each other, mirroring each other's smiles and postures. One of them waves a dripping red talon in the air to illustrate a point, and a second later the other one tries it on for size. They are edging ever closer, snuffling up musk and chemicals that are being secreted for each other's benefit, certainly not for mine. It really is time to let them get on with it. And besides, I won't have to listen to any more of this.

' . . . the artist has just as valid a claim on a dead body as any pathologist or surgeon. We will make the flesh live for ever! We will find meaning in decay, the deconstruction of the outmoded idea of individual reality . . .'

There's more, and Sasha is drinking in every word.

'I've got to go,' I say, standing up so suddenly that my tall, thin stool scrapes across the hard, shiny floor. 'Leave you the keys?'

I dangle the taxi keys in front of Sasha and watch her greedy little eyes shine at the thought of driving her girlfriend around in a cab then doing it on the back seat. Or on the floor. Or on the aptly named jump seat. Or maybe even while driving, getting Cathy to scuff her authentic 1960s nylons on the rubber floormat while she buries her face between Sasha's legs as my little tigress struggles to keep the cab on the road and her cute little peaked chauffeur's cap from sliding down over her dreamy sex-smudged face. Well, there could be some projection of my own hopes and dreams here, but there is no doubt that the poor old cab won't know what's hit it once those two get going. And I, a mere male, shouldn't even be here any more, but my morose nod of farewell has not been accepted.

'Remember we planned to go on that boat trip before all this madness started?' says Sasha.

I had forgotten actually, what with one thing and another, but I suppose it all fits in with Sasha's childish desire to find the last piece of her jigsaw, the who-did-what-to-whom part fetish of hers that you would think that recent events had made even more irrelevant.

'Richard will be there,' I say.

'Yeah, you can push him over the side,' she says with a beaming smile. 'You're good at that.'

This reference to a strategic drowning I was involved in last year is incautious to say the least. We shouldn't really be discussing old murders in the presence of a stranger, although perhaps it's only me who thinks of Cathy as a stranger.

We are probably working from two different scripts, as usual, but one thing I am indisputably good at is flouncing out of the house and mooching around for hours on end. It's far too long since I did that.

'Yeah, I'll see you at Chelsea Harbour,' I say. 'I can see you want to talk art. And so on.'

She can't suppress a grin. 'And so on,' she says, quickly raising and lowering her eyebrows. As I turn to go, the blather starts up again, exactly where it left off with mutilated cadavers, flesh canvases and the artist as mortician. They are so wrapped up in each other that they don't even notice me bundling the folded-up arm into my shoulder bag as I leave.

13

WELL, I'M NOT jealous. And even if I was I am at last alone and free to do what I'm really good at; walking around while arguing with myself – out loud, more often than not. Try as I might, I can't drug myself with newsprint or the attempt to read other people's lives from their passage through the Soho streets. Only alcohol or heroin could quell this sort of anxiety, and all I have is the Sunset Strip Club – the only Soho sex show where you can sit down without receiving a fruit juice cocktail and a bill for three hundred quid. Stan the doorman is a jazz fan and lets musicians in free, so I don't tell him I have upgraded myself to the position of personal therapist's consultant. After I have nodded my way through his monologue, somehow maintaining a smile even while Sasha's treachery is gnawing a hole in my heart, I take the stairs down to the temple of Venus.

It's like a little review cinema down there, but the audience is considerably more attentive than a bunch of jaded hacks wondering why they only make movies for teenagers these days. I take my place among the lone men studiously ignoring each other. The dancer comes so close that it is possible to discern the real odours of her body even from under the cloud of cloying perfume she is drenched in. Somewhere inside all of that there is even a hint of the grubby sweat-stained money that is nestling in her garter. And that *is* filthy.

The artiste is young, intelligent, attractive and a competent contortionist, but my mind is not really on the cleanly shaven opening gyrating less than six inches before my face, or even on the cute mole beside it. I'm too busy fantasising about Cathy. Not the usual stuff; more that she might meet with some sort of accidental death. An overdose, perhaps. Or a bondage accident. Some of those masks can be really dangerous, you know. So they tell me. Skulduggery of this order needs a little help from the original Skaldi herself – a dark flint-eyed Viking goddess whom even Sasha would think twice about tangling with – and with this in mind I stuff some tenners into the dancer's stocking tops. This buys me a genuine smile and some specially wiggly bits, obviously a sign that I will prevail against Cathy. But then the 1970s Muzak dribbles to a close, the dancer scampers offstage and the spell is broken.

I ring for a mini-cab to take me to Chelsea Harbour. It's a surprise when the driver turns out to be white and thirtyish, but Phil Collins on Capital FM is no less irritating than the insistent rattle and thump of a dance station. And the driver wants to talk. He has a new theory, something to do with large amounts of traffic causing the jam we are sitting in, but does little to develop it in his opening five-minute address. Then he gives me some reheated items from the *Sun* and *Talk Radio* and a lot of stuff about stress. Throughout, I behave like an expensive therapist, saying almost nothing except an occasional grunt, all the while reflecting that at least shrinks have got the patient's fee to look forward to at the end of a session. Cab driving must be the only form of therapy where the patient gets paid.

At Chelsea Harbour there are about thirty party perves waiting on the landing stage. Sasha and Cathy are all giggles and quick little hugs until they see me approach. They are surrounded by a small stooping cluster of flabby men in leather harnesses who are queuing up, hoping to be abused. Sasha is already a legend among some of these submissives. Every time her gleaming silver boots take a few steps her entourage of overgrown slugs slithers along in her wake. I stand as upright as possible while I scrutinise the lovebirds for evidence of carnal knowledge.

Sasha looks a little worried, while Cathy is harder to read, her face ripple-free, her eyes as unreadable as the dark oily waters of the Thames. She could make more of an effort considering the circumstances. It's not as if I was expecting a neatly written thank-you letter for lending her Sasha for a few hours, but the correct open-marriage etiquette when returning a life-partner to the rightful owner is surely to attempt some fake hippie lurve vibe.

Cathy is wearing boots and a shiny black rubber corset which will no doubt fall apart after a few wearings. Her punitive access-ories include a rubber riding crop. Sasha is all rubbered up too, her breasts coated in spray-on latex into which she has sprinkled some silver stardust. Someone has sprinkled some happiness into her shimmering eyes too, and I don't have to look very far for the prime suspect.

Sasha has an extra eyebrow-piercing too. I wonder who put that in. And what they did while the piercing rush flashed through her veins and how intense it was knowing that this was the first time and . . . I'm going to stop thinking about that now. I'm going to ignore what their underwear in a clammy tangled heap on the floor might have looked like. Or smelled like. Or the sort of positions a trained martial artist like Cathy could twist her lean dark body into. It's time to put that to one side and move on. And not to speculate whether I will find any fresh crop marks or scratches or scars or even burns on Sasha's body. I might not even be seeing it again, for all I know.

'What have you done with the arm?' whispers Sasha urgently.

I pat my shoulder bag and nod reassuringly.

'You should *not* have taken it,' says Cathy. 'I want it *back*.'

We are in the middle of what looks like being a long staring match when Sasha tells us both to grow up before stomping off to the other end of the pier, inadvertently treading on the fingers of a naked man who smiles weakly in gratitude. Cathy walks slowly and gracefully after her, the floor-level dross rolling to one side to allow her through. Just as I'm breathing deeply and unclenching my fists, I notice that another very bad advert for fetishism and middle-aged men in general is walking towards me. Ignoring my grim demeanour, he greets me warmly.

Jimmy Allen. And his bushy beard, authentic pirate's outfit and foaming pewter tankard of best British ale. I look round quickly but there's no escape. We have to wait here till the boat arrives. Jimmy is still talking, of course, as he would be if I were to burst into flames then crumble into charred hanks of black, blistered meat in front of him. He is telling me about flogging in the British Navy while Sasha's shining silver boots clump away with Cathy in hot pursuit. I am trying to work out if that is their first lovers' tiff while Jimmy continues with the ramifications of forehand or backhand application and the derivation of cat-of-nine-tails.

As he walks, listing well to starboard, he seems to create his own exclusion zone – a little cloud of beer, beard and boredom. In no time at all he is back. I have obviously been marked for death by some malevolent sprite, perhaps even Hugh himself.

The sight of a dominant man in an SS uniform sets Jimmy off again. 'I can't believe that Nazi uniforms have been allowed in s/m space,' he says.

'Really?' I say, more concerned about the frolicking perves who should be waiting till we get on the boat before the first crack of the whip. The police are always strangely touchy about other uniform freaks with handcuffs. Meanwhile, Jimmy has decided that I am letting the side down.

'Bit boring, isn't it?' he says, giving me the once-over. 'Leather jacket and a T-shirt? Hardly a fetish at all. I mean, with your bald head and that shoulder bag you look more like a New Age postman. Drink?'

'I don't drink.'

'I only asked. No need to bite my head off. It's Sam Smith's. Lovely stuff.'

'I know. I gave up.'

'Oh, one of those. Oh, well. Cheers.'

At least the boat has arrived, and once we have all been herded aboard − literally in some cases − I find Sasha on the top deck. She looks especially cute in rubber and a nautical white-peaked cap. A fat naked man is face down at her feet as I scowl my greeting.

'That's the church that features in *Alfie*,' she tells me, pulling on my arm to get me to look in the right direction. I glare at the church briefly before shrugging her arm off.

'Didn't you see the movie? With Michael Caine?' she says.

I grip the rail hard enough to hurt myself then stare at the moon for a while, ignoring her slight pout and imploring eyes. I've seen all that before.

'Where did you get the white cap from?' I say finally. I've nearly got my voice under control.

'The captain gave it to me. Do you like it?'

'Very fetching. Does Cathy like it?'

'So that's what all this is about. We didn't fuck.'

'But you will soon.'

'Oh, what do you know? We want to collaborate on an art project.'

'Really? It's the first time I've ever heard it called that before.'

'It's cute. You being jealous.' She smooths her sticky rubber skirt over her bare legs and smiles wickedly. 'It's so sweaty, this outfit,' she says.

I nod helplessly. You might as well give in – it's quicker.

'When we get back you can peel these knickers off, and my juices are going to spill right out.'

Very nice, but having Hugh's arm in my shoulder bag is making it hard to concentrate on anything else. It's almost like it's alive, as if it might fight its way out of my shoulder bag and scamper off to the nearest policeman, pointing at us and shouting: 'They did it! Them over there!'

But despite what Sasha, and dope and acid and the mushrooms occasionally tell me, inanimate objects have no life. I should be worrying about whether it will be Alice, Richard or Cathy who will betray us. After all, any one of them could break down, find Jesus in recovery and then confess all as part of the healing process. I'm reasonably convinced I can trust Sasha, but she was raised Catholic. There's always the danger she might crack one day.

'Wouldn't you like to blow that lot up?' I say, as yet another expense-account feeding barn appears on the starboard bow.

'You can't turn the clock back, you old hippie,' she says.

I think about pointing out that she doesn't call me Granddad so much now that she has passed thirty but decide not to risk any 'playful' retaliatory action.

'Didn't you have some method for that?' I ask. 'Turning back time?'

Her eyes light up 'Visualise an eight-legged sunwheel . . .'

'It's a swastika. Call a spade a spade.'

' . . . a sunwheel, a right-handed sunwheel and rotate it. If you're late for something it holds back time.'

Which could be why she's always late. I don't believe in right-handed sunwheels. She's still waiting for me to nod or say yes so I do both as best I can before stealing an embrace I haven't really earned. The lights reflected in the Thames are also to be seen in her glistening eyes, until the kiss develops and she screws her eyes shut. I decide closed eyes means eternal love and the rejection of Cathy and all her works, then close my eyes to dream a little bit longer.

As the kiss continues I'm hoping that the footsteps on the stairs are Cathy's, but it's just the captain, a weathered old salt with slicked-down grey hair and eyes that have been suspended in some solution of whisky and nicotine. The sight of the fat slave fills him with revulsion, but then he has a slow lingering letch over Sasha. Until he catches my eye.

'Thank God for a pretty girl,' he says.

Sasha bristles at that but manages to stay calm.

'It's full of poofs kissing each other down there.'

Oh dear, my little tigress will have something to say about that.

'So what's your obsession?' says Sasha, handing him back his cap. 'Let me guess. Page-three bimbos and spanking. Homosexuality is an abomination before the Lord. Just in case you ever find out you like it, you fucking old hypocrite.'

'Swearing. Very ladylike,' he says, as if this was a devastating put-down. 'I don't have to take that from you.'

'You going make us walk the plank, you old fart?'

'This is my boat . . .'

'And what? There's more of us.'

'Steady on, babe,' I begin, before remembering that 'babe', or That Word as it is now known, was banned in a previous peace treaty I had forgotten about. That three-day conflict had been resolved by the outlawing of the B-word and other demeaning endearments. I think I was just supposed to say 'sir' eventually.

'Right, that's it,' he says, and storms off to do something or other that will show us.

It takes a while to chivvy the fat man down the stairs, but eventually we get rid of him with a mixture of harsh words and boot leather, which leaves us alone with the moonlight and the Thames. Sasha wants to get all cuddly again. Or huggy. Or cuggly, her special word for those clingy moments she values even more than a sound thrashing followed by a brisk dousing with red-wine vinegar. It's a good moment to catch her off-guard.

'You know Stewart James is on board,' I say, dropping the name of a certain bondage guru and battle re-enactment fanatic, the sort of man Jimmy Allen might regard as being obsessed. 'I wonder if I should ask Stewart about the mask Hugh died in,' I say. 'He designed it, didn't he?'

She smiles thinly, mostly to herself. She is avoiding my eyes. 'Oh, yes?' she says.

'Didn't he tell you about being extra-careful with the mask? Because of the danger of suffocation?'

Sasha is still looking at the lights of the South Bank complex reflected in the Thames. 'Stewart? I took some acting lessons from him once.'

She closes her eyes and shivers. Sasha doesn't like to talk about when she tried to be a real actress. It was one of the few times when her sorcery was not enough.

'Isn't he a vicious old queen who is a bit hard on women?' I say, recalling the inevitable gossip.

'No! He actually likes women. Many *gay* men do.'

There is a pause while I decide not to bother trying to float the theory that heterosexual men really do like women. Even I couldn't get away with that one.

'I'm sure he told you how to use that mask safely,' I say, just a little irony creeping into my voice.

Sasha starts to talk very quickly. 'Hugh had loads of those masks. He had an enormous collection. How was I to know which one was which? And why would I want to kill him off? We earned a fortune from him.'

It sounds very convincing. Except it's coming out as if rehearsed. And why isn't she annoyed if I'm accusing her of murder? Probably because we have been here before. The ghost of her first husband is never too far away from these little discussions about the sanctity of human life. Sasha apparently helped Spider Black out of his misery at his own request, which is fair enough, but some people take the view that thirty-one is a little young for euthanasia.

When I lift my head out of my hands I notice that a whipping trestle has been set up on the lower decks. A long but orderly queue quickly forms while a number of dominants jostle for position at the head of the line. Cathy is elbowing her way to prominence as the Houses of Parliament appear. A man with white whip-scars over his entire body kisses Cathy's feet while she looks up at us, swishing a cat-of-nine-tails through the air.

'Not like that . . .' begins Jimmy.

Cathy says something to him that hits him like a bucket of cold water and then delivers the first lash softly, to warm the skin and prepare the recipient for the long, slow journey ahead. But the next one wrings a screwed-up face even from the sea-

soned submissive tethered to the trestle. Soon she has managed
to break the skin, and a number of busybodies are pointing out
that this is illegal, even between consenting adults. Cathy just
puts even more into the next stroke, the trickle of blood on the
blushing cheeks growing darker and thicker. Sasha is entranced,
watching her pet puss in action, but I want to know if she killed
Hugh.

'You put the mask on him. If you knew it would kill him . . .'

Sasha is looking at me blankly.

'I mean, some people, some nitpickers, might say this made
you a murderer.'

'Would you care if it did?'

'You know I do.'

'And these guys you kill in pubs because you're drunk? What's
that called again?'

'It was one guy and it was your idea, I seem to recall.'

' "I seem to recall". That's a good one. You will never
recall anything about that time. You were too busy crying into
your beer. I had to sort everything out. Then you killed JC. Not
by accident. Sober.'

'Who misses him?'

'I see.' She puts on the Cro-Magnon face, which means she's
going to imitate my voice.

'Well, I done him in, your honour, but no one liked him.
Duh!' She is holding both hands out and pulling a silly face.

'Can't you speak without waving your hands about?'

Her reply is a single solitary digit held upright, much more
eloquent than words could ever be. A little while later she says,
'Why do we bother? We have nothing in common.'

'At least we both want to shag Cathy,' I say, as the dome of
St Paul's appears.

'Hmm. Looks kinda nice in the moonlight, doesn't it?' she says, as if we haven't been arguing.

'I knew someone who leaped off the Whispering Gallery,' I say, as I always do at this point.

'Wow. Must have made a mess.'

'Yeah. If only you could have photographed it.'

The bitterness is back in my voice, but Sasha gives me a look which says that the subject of transgressive art is closed for the moment.

'You know why I think you might have killed Hugh?' I say. 'Because you're jealous. I've done more people than you have.'

'You cretin! That's . . . just *so* wrong!'

'Why are you screaming at me, then?'

For a moment it looks like I'm going to have my ankles badly nipped, but instead she decides to turn away with an exasperated sigh. There is a space here for me to press home my advantage, but just then some horrid 1980s techno starts up and a group of men in leather harnesses start prancing about and hopping from one foot to the other. Now and again they hit each other with soft leather floggers and rattle the bells on their boots.

'Oh, no!' says Sasha, hand over her mouth.

'Oh, yes!' I say as the full horror hits me. 'It's morris dancing.'

'What's morris dancing?'

'Trust me. You don't want to know.'

'Why are they jumping up and down?'

'It's part of our folk heritage.'

'It's cute.'

'It's sick.'

'Hmm. I rang Richard. He's wants us to go to the houseboat,' she says, avoiding my eyes.

She's trying to slip this past me while I'm distracted by the morris dancing. She is well aware that I don't want to stay up another night. Or go play with Richard again.

'I'm falling apart, Sasha. I can't do this.'

'He's got some toot. And we could start our initiation.'

'Yes,' I say, knowing all too well what this might mean. One of the perks of having your own black magic sect is devising initiation ordeals and, on occasion, these have been known to contain a sexual element. Now and again. I'm not at all sure if I'm up to an encounter with Thor's hammer, the huge double-headed dildo Richard keeps for new recruits.

'Is Cathy coming?' I say.

Sasha's smile tells me that I didn't manage to sound neutral. 'She's got punters tomorrow. And she wants that arm back more than anything else.'

'Let her come and get it, then.'

'You're so childish.'

'We need to throw it away. We do not need to play pathetic art-school games with a bit of dead flesh. Besides, just think of the fun Richard is going to have with it. He's probably never been fisted by a dead guy before.'

'That's brilliant!' says Sasha. 'He'll love that!'

'Oh, well, perhaps he could write some of his visceral poetry about it. "Your cold hand touches me, somewhere deep inside".'

' "Now you're up my asshole, I have no more secrets to hide",' says Sasha, essaying a little dance step to go with her couplet. She's always happy when she's being creative.

'Speaking of secrets,' she says. 'I have to find out who the Dungeonmaster's Apprentice is.'

'Yes,' I say, as I always will, I suppose.

'I feel lucky tonight,' she says.

'Hmm. Let's hope Richard won't rupture our colons during the opening invocation of Beelzebub.'

'Play your cards right and you might get to rupture his,' says Sasha. 'Look, we're nearly there.'

The big wedding-cake edifice of the Royal Naval College is looming up on the starboard bow. As we approach there is a mad scramble to scrape up the wreckage – human and subhuman – pack up the scourges and swab the blood off the decks. Keys are being frantically jiggled in handcuffs, and cool, soothing cream is being slathered over hot smarting bottoms. The terrified bar staff are telling their customers that the bar is shut with an even more triumphant note than usual as the captain blusters an ultimatum at the event's organiser as we dock.

'Well, if we are going to Richard's, maybe you had better kiss your girlfriend goodbye,' I say, sounding bitter and hurt instead of cool and detached.

'Good idea,' she says and flounces off to do just that.

I am still blundering about in a rage five minutes later and, while looking for a handy cat to kick, I manage to upset a small rickety table loaded with Jimmy's junk – crops, whips, flogging guides. The collision raises a fond smile on Sasha's face for she is familiar with the sound of breaking furniture. Somehow she gets me on her side again. We are going to Richard's. There will be no sleep, for ever – if she has her way, which she usually does. Unless her plans go wrong and we somehow both get to the end of this incarnation a lot sooner than planned. Something about that wicked skewed smile is telling me that I was right not to bother with a pension. I'm never going to live to spend it.

14

THE RICKETY GANGPLANK and the tiny doorway make it difficult to get on or inside Richard's houseboat, even for those who can manage to walk in a straight line without careering into the nearest breakable object. I clamber in without the usual pratfall but then step in Richard's washing-up bowl. No dishes break, but the ensuing chortles and snickers do nothing to calm me down. The interior is dark and dank, lit by candles in what I hope are imitation skulls. Richard greets us with his familiar death's-head grin.

'You look divine,' he says to Sasha. 'And you look drab as ever,' he says to me.

'Is Hugh still here?' I ask. 'Or did you manage to raise him from the dead?'

He doesn't rise to the bait. Nor is he even looking at me when he replies. 'No such luck,' he says. 'Hugh is still with us. You know, some guests never know when to take their leave.'

I'm surprised to see that Alice and Richard are sat round a

table eating. They don't look the sort to play happy families. The warm glow from the candles flatters Alice, who looks a little better than the skulls. Clothing fetishists will need to know that she is wearing some prewar sixth-form schoolgirl stuff and that underneath she will probably have the appropriate underwear, but the only important detail is that she looks very drawn and very haggard.

I am the last person she ever wants to see in any circumstances, but for once she cannot blitz me with one of her looks because we have her at a disadvantage. She looks especially shifty as we pull up a beer crate around the dusty table, perhaps ashamed to be seen doing anything so mundane as eating. And especially not the sort of hearty stew they are tucking in to. There's just time to ruin the rest of it if I get in quick.

'Surprised you can stomach that with Hugh still on board,' I say.

Alice throws her fork down in disgust and reaches for her cigarettes. Richard, stripped to the waist and his hair tied behind him in some ludicrous foppish bow, carries on eating.

'Will you join us?' he says, taut muscles moving around under his tight flesh as he waves his silver fork at us.

'No, thanks.'

'It's a shame Stanley isn't around,' I say. 'You could have fed Hugh to the dog.' Richard's fork pauses on the way up to his mouth.

'I already have,' he says, nodding at Alice.

Richard looks straight at me as he swallows a glistening morsel of something or other.

Alice's face crumples into its constituent wrinkles. 'That's revolting, Richard,' she says.

'You ate it,' he replies. 'I thought it was quite nice myself. A little fatty perhaps. But that was Hugh for you.'

'Oh, *do* shut up, Richard. Even you would never . . .'

Richard dabs at his mouth delicately with a monogrammed linen napkin then walks over to a cupboard. Once he knows we are all watching him he throws it open to reveal Hugh, who is missing crucial bits of his stomach and thighs.

'So that's what the smell is,' says Sasha.

Richard's smile widens. '*Eternity* by Hugh Dick,' he says. 'Haunting, isn't it?'

Alice bolts for the door but has to puke before she gets there. It's a most inelegant spectacle, what with the weeping and the retching and a bit of screaming thrown in. And now we have what might be second-hand fricassee of Hugh all over the floor I'm starting to feel a tad queasy myself.

'You wouldn't,' says Sasha to Richard.

'It's not even illegal, actually,' he says. 'We could eat the evidence.'

Alice remains on all fours, shaking and weeping as strands of her hair mingle with the mess she is making. Sasha walks over and examines the top of Alice's head, quite a lot of which is grey.

'You need to do your roots,' she says.

I would go over for a gloat myself but I'm so tired. None of us is looking our best presently, but it's fair to say that Alice seems to be feeling it more than most. Otherwise she would never have fallen for this pathetic trick of Richard's. I can't help noticing that Hugh is now wearing a pair of white frilly panties. And lipstick.

'I suppose he's a cheap date,' I say.

'Don't worry,' says Richard. 'I haven't been interfering with him, if that's what you think. I didn't like him when he was warm, thank you very much.'

'Yes. And how could you fuck anyone who wasn't putting up a fight?' I say.

Richard just cackles, like the horror-movie caricature he is fast becoming, then selects a CD from a small dusty pile of trodden-on stuff by his chair. Judging the mood of solemn remembrance and quiet contemplation perfectly, he selects some Third Reich marching songs. These turn out to be rousing stuff but not what we need right now.

'Real dance music,' says Richard, tossing me a catalogue of Hitler kitsch offered by 'Siegfried of England'.

'How did you get like this, Richard?' says Sasha, shaking her head.

It's something I've occasionally pondered, and the best I could come up with is a traumatic childhood event, a stock-market crash, perhaps. 'I blame the parents,' I say, as I usually do.

But for once this feeble jest has some point. Richard looks less omnipotent than usual; a virulent scowl has disfigured his features. The aura of invincibility slips for a moment until an especially demonic smile slithers back on to his face.

'Have you got your gun, dear?' he says to Sasha. 'Or did you give it to your bit of rough?'

Sasha looks at me and I wish she hadn't. We have two bullets left, and with my trembling hand I really don't know if that's enough. I pat the pocket the gun's in and wait to see if Richard has some bigger, better weapon to pull on us.

'Did you bring the money?' he says.

'Yeah. But what are we going to get for it? asks Sasha.

'Everything you will ever need,' he says.

'Right now, we are being threatened by the Dungeonmaster's Apprentice. Would you know who that is?'

'Of course. Don't you?'

I really can't tell from the silly face he is pulling if he knows or not.

'He's the man behind the Black Order. Once you have joined

us you will know,' he says. 'That's if you've got the gonads to undergo our little initiative test.'

I look at Alice, who is smiling very tightly at me. She sucks in some smoke then leisurely taps the ash off the end of her cigarette. I might have known she would be a card-carrying member.

'Why would we want to join?' I say, while Sasha hisses at me.

Richard smiles broadly and settles down to enjoy the sound of his own voice again. 'You know how much the average club promoter makes. The Dungeonmaster has all that plus he doesn't have to split the take with whoever's running the door. There are no adverts, no taxes. You just need some millionaires you can give the treatment.'

'The treatment?'

He laughs, long enough to make my blood boil. Don't I know *anything*?

'Hypnotise them,' he says. 'Put some mushrooms in their drink. Long, drawn-out rituals in a scented, darkened room. More to the point, shag them stupid for the first time in their life.'

'Sex and drugs.'

'And rock and roll,' says Sasha.

'Even better, there is no rock and roll,' says Alice.

'Plenty of Wagner, I'll bet,' I say.

'The adept sees too clearly to be politically correct,' says Richard, sounding like he is recycling one of his favourite little mottoes. 'The first part of your test is easy,' he continues. 'You just have to drive slowly through Brixton wearing some of Alice's genuine Nazi uniforms. Think you're up to that?'

As he will never know where we have driven once we have left him I say yes.

'You will have to film the event, of course,' he says. 'Just to prove you have done it.'

I look at Sasha, who is all excited now something pointlessly dangerous is going to happen.

'And you have to have the money,' says Richard.

Sasha counts out the cash, avoiding my eyes because all this is news to me.

'Six hundred and sixty-six pounds,' he says, as if just saying this number out loud was daring or dangerous.

'You never grew up, did you?' I say.

'And neither might you. If you displease me. So listen. And I will tell you the rules of our little game.'

15

MINI-CABBING IT to Chelsea to retrieve our cab would normally be a grim and turgid task, but this time the driver doesn't get a word in edgeways – must be something to do with the pharmaceutical cocaine we shot before the journey. Yes, we did use clean needles, thanks for asking. Sasha brought her own, making it likely that she knew all about this little treat in advance, a suspicion confirmed by the casual nonchalance with which she walked to the sink to puke after the injection.

She's obviously keeping other secrets from me, but I don't care about that, or about anything else, until the coke wears off. On my return another hit gets us all into the cab for a drive south to Alice's place. Halfway around the South Circular Richard starts to babble and it soon becomes clear we need restraints. Or we need Cathy. Alice and Sasha aren't really going to be enough to stop him waving his arms around or kicking at the partition or exposing himself out of the window. While I'm usually in favour of alternative lifestyles, a traffic jam in Blackheath is no place to unsheath a heavily pierced member. As he starts to wave his pride and joy out of the window it soon becomes clear that he is up to his old tricks of hanging two-pound weights off the end of his Prince Albert piercing. I am already aware from countless viewings of his favourite party trick that the crocodile clips will keep the weight in place, as long as his flesh holds out, but I'm not sure my nerves can stand the teardrop-shaped weight clanking repeatedly into the cab door.

There is also the possibility that he might be trying to repel magickal attack by some other sinister sorcerer. Ritual masturbation is often an aid to enchantment – that's their excuse anyway – but he seems most likely to invoke the local bill if he continues to dangle that thing out of the window. Not much later he is back to screaming and cowering on the floor, and it's beginning to look like he has picked the wrong number in the LSD lottery.

'Do something!' wails Sasha.

I pick up my cosh from under the seat and slam the brakes on, which throws him off-balance. As I draw close to him I can tell that he doesn't even know who I am any more. It's also clear that I had better get a good shot in with the cosh, but it's difficult to get near him as his long legs are scything through the air in front of him. The blows I am landing will bruise up nicely, but I need to get at his knees or elbows, and his skull is still about six feet away from me. It's not until one of Sasha's shiny silver Doctor Martens connects with his jaw that it is possible to land a blow on his knee. While he is coping with that I try to get at his elbow, but he is still doing his whirling dervish act. Although he is raving away, using all of his lung capacity to express something or other, he seems impervious to pain. By the time I club my way up to the skull it still takes two shots to put him out. Once you start something like that it's hard to stop, but combined screeching from Sasha and Alice ruins that particular avenue of enjoyment. I drive on in a sulk until we reach Alice's semi-detached house, tucked away in the faceless suburban wastes of Streatham.

Hefting Richard inside isn't easy, but at least it gives me the chance to bang his head on the pavement as we go. The house smells equally of floor polish and the sort of herbs your village wise women use to stupefy themselves after a hard evening dancing round their cauldrons. Alice has obviously put a lot of effort into creating this artificial 1930s environment of blistered buttocks and toasted muffins, but whether she feels any better as a result is debatable. Perhaps I shouldn't judge. I'm not well myself, you know.

We are greeted by an English rose complete with porcelain skin, a red flush to her cheeks and raven-black ringlets framing a pleasantly chubby face. For once there is little tension between the inner world of the fantasist and the external reality of bad acting and human frailty as maid and mistress act out a familiar charade for our benefit. Alice is perfect in the role of an imperious old boot as she delivers a long reprimand to the maid in the sort of English that now seems to have fallen into disuse. Or desuetude, as Alice would probably have it.

'Your cap is not starched and you have been warned about wearing outdoor shoes in the house,' she continues, cranking up her fake posh accent for the part. 'Have you been punished today?'

'No, madame.'

'Wait for me in the scullery.'

I watch the maid carefully as she leaves, but she is either a good actress or a very sincere amateur. Her performance is flawless. There is an unpleasant proprietorial air to Alice's triumphant smile as the door closes. Once she realises there isn't going to be a round of applause, she starts telling us what to do in exactly the same voice she used on her maid. I knew this was going to happen and try to make this apparent to Sasha while we are being instructed in how to treat her precious uniforms. Sasha is being uncharacteristically servile for the moment, which is making me wonder what she has planned for later when we find out the identity of the Dungeonmaster's Apprentice. For Sasha this whole thing is probably about the skinned cat. She won't rest till whoever did that has been skinned alive themselves. At the very least.

'These uniforms are very valuable. You will be careful,' says Alice, her flint face making clear that this is not a question.

'You're really into this giving orders stuff, aren't you?' says Sasha. 'Are you a Nazi too?'

Alice stiffens and blitzes Sasha with a haughty stare, but when she sees it's not going to get her anywhere she answers the question.

'Richard is not a Nazi,' she says. 'And neither am I. But some hierarchies are useful. You must learn to obey before you can exercise authority. Something my maid must learn. Now you must excuse me. I have to chastise her.'

Inside what Alice has insisted we call the robing-room the air is heavy with the scent of mothballs. Sasha would join any club or society that let her dress up so she is happy for the moment as she tries out different outfits, eventually settling for a white shirt and tight knickers that mimic the ones the Bundes Deutsch Mädels wore for their sports displays. The purple fingernails and gleaming scarlet lipstick may not be authentic, but they certainly set the blood racing. With her lopsided smile and knowing eyes, the kit looks anything but healthy and outdoors, although she has plaited her hair and twirled the plaits around her ears, a typically earnest Germanic fashion that has rightly been ignored by the rest of the world.

'Well?' she says.

I'm still straining my ears to hear any of the slow ritual correction that should be taking place around now, but it's easy enough to tell Sasha she looks gorgeous. She wants more, though.

'You look stunning,' I say, meaning it. 'Should be illegal really, you in a Nazi schoolgirl costume.'

'Does it really suit me?' she says, twirling coquettishly. When she comes to rest, a twisted smile is firmly in place and her eyes have that special glitter. I used to have the extra kick of knowing that this face was just for me, but as it has recently been thrown open to the general public my own smile is a little strained.

'Come on,' she says. 'Don't sulk. Cathy will be gone soon. She's too in love with herself.'

'You might really go for something you can't have.'

'No. I kicked unrequited love a long time ago.'

Really? I don't believe a word of it, but there is no point dwelling on it. Especially as she is starting to adopt the teenage tomboy mannerisms that go with her schoolgirl role. But there's no time to take advantage of that because she is busy pinning supposedly authentic Third Reich badges on her shirt.

She's probably safe, though, because anyone we meet is more likely to be too busy slitting my throat to notice her little swastika badges. I am now wearing what might be an SS general's uniform. Even if it's a fake it's still likely to be a talking point in Brixton. I notice that Richard's spare black trousers 'for dwarfs', as he put it, are still too long. As I can't see the little woman rushing for the nearest sewing machine to run me up a perfect set of turn-ups I bodge some hand-folded ones. The results are either lopsided or fashionably asymmetrical, but I doubt if anyone is going to get past the peaked cap and the swastika armband anyway.

Downstairs again we find Alice fussing over Richard in the kitchen. Once Alice has turned her back I rest my entire weight on his knuckles for an instant. Internal bruising should see to it that he will not be invoking anything by magical masturbation for some considerable time. Not with that hand anyway.

'You had better hope he doesn't remember what happened,' says Alice, filling up a bucket with water at the sink.

'You asked me to do it!' I say.

'Don't whine, man. You really are pathetic!'

Alice then douses Richard full in the face with the entire contents of the bucket.

He takes a few minutes to moan and groan but then a swig of brandy, four aspirin and a nice cup of tea flavoured with organic honey get him back to his old obnoxious self.

'This is a great day for you two,' he says, managing a smile despite his aches and pains.

'The first step on the path to real achievement. Once you join the Black Order you will want for nothing. Drugs, women, men, small boys, melons. Anything your heart could desire.'

'Hollowed-out aubergine?' says Sasha, pulling her white knee-socks up and checking that her shirt is well tucked in.

'Aubergines aren't long enough to take me, my dear,' he says. 'You should get rid of him and try me sometime.'

He winks at her. Then at me. It really is time to offer him my card and arrange to meet somewhere at dawn where we can settle this like gentlemen, but I settle for a quiet sneer instead. He just blows me another kiss, which hurts more than a chinning would have done.

'*Blutreinigung*?' says Sasha uncertainly, as she noses through the herbal tea collection.

You would think that the ritual dismemberment of Hugh Dick and the wearing of Nazi uniforms through Brixton would take precedence over foreign herbal teas, but then she has a different set of priorities from most people. She's always looking for some pill or potion that will cure her of whatever dreadful allergy or ailment she has got this week.

'It cleans the blood,' I say. 'You're very keen on pure blood, aren't you, Richard?'

'Blood and soil,' he intones, which causes Alice to twitch her lips briefly.

I ask for a nettle tea, not because I want one but because I want to see the maid faff about at our behest. As she assembles the herbs, the pot, a strainer, cups and suchlike it is clear from her stiff-legged walk that Alice is a hard taskmaster.

What with one thing and another – Sasha's outfit, the maid's smouldering eyes and blushing cheeks, both sets – I feel the need to discuss recent developments with Sasha somewhere private, somewhere we could be undisturbed, but this isn't the time or the place. Alice seems to have the same internal surveillance system that Richard has, little security cameras poking out from the ceiling in most rooms, so we will have to wait.

And something else is happening. The shape of Sasha's head is changing, she is grinning mightily and a strange shimmer through my stomach alerts me that Richard has mixed in some psilocybin mushrooms with the drinks he gave us at his place.

'It's mushrooms,' I say to Richard, who looks bigger and even more frightening now.

'Better hope it is,' he says.

The doorbell rings and we all freeze. This really is an especially inconvenient moment for the police to arrive. Alice glides quickly to the answerphone and presses a button.

A Jamaican voice makes the tinny little speaker rattle.

'We want to talk about Jesus Christ. Have you been saved?'

Richard's shoulders start shaking, and then he's motioning me to the door. 'Go and answer it,' he is saying.

His eyebrows are begging me to do it, and Sasha is cackling

too. I think back to that little business last Easter. Sasha and I actually are one of a very small select band who have been crucified and then lived to tell the tale. We actually are 'born again'. I go to the door to share this knowledge but, just before I open it, I can see in the mirror that the peaked cap really balances the surplus jowls that comfort eating have bestowed on me. As the light catches the twin sun runes of the SS symbol I am not entirely sure who it is grinning back at me. It's definitely not me, whoever that is, but then I remember why I try not to look in the mirror too long any more, especially not on mushrooms – you never know who is coming out to play.

The doorbell rings again, and it really would be a shame to disappoint such an insistent evangelist. I fling the door open and blitz the guy with a pair of glittering eyes and a click of my heels. He has a fat round face and white hair – someone's granddad, perhaps.

'So! You are here to join our party?' I say, borrowing Richard's stage German accent.

The guy's lower jaw practically falls off, then his eyes blow up to the size of soup plates. I wish I had a monocle to flourish, but I can still take the cap off and let my bald head glint in the streetlights. He recovers quickly, of course, having Jesus and a host of cherubim and seraphim on his side. He starts to laugh, a lovely honey-flavoured deep baritone. I have to smile myself, now the mushrooms are giving me the giggles.

'Join us, brother,' he says, handing me a tract which I accept, closing the door gently.

Well, well, well. He thought it was just fancy dress. Which is what it is; Richard hasn't a clue really. This is going to be less of an ordeal than a laugh, a bit of a spree, a giggle. And just keep telling yourself that, my boy, for soon it will be time for the festivities to commence.

Sasha is still haggling with Richard. She has her hands on her hips and he is not smiling for once.

'Look, you little bitch,' he is saying. 'Fact is, there is a lot of fake money about. How can I trust you?' He's holding her money up to the light, a pointless wind-up, but she starts to seethe anyway. Sasha always gets angry in retail outlets every time they test her money. Maybe it's because they didn't pick her to be the picture on the money. I mean, who is queen around here anyway? Some old bag who has raised a family of mutants or the real thing?

'Shut up,' says Sasha, to me. I really should stop giggling, but it feels so good.

'Membership of the Black Order is the key to worldly power,' says Richard. 'The keys to the kingdom.'

Sasha and I look at each other. We know we want it. We are, to use Richard's useful little phrase, 'gagging for it'. But do we want to be dragged out of the cab and kicked to death in Brixton?

'The Black Order . . .' he begins, but I don't want to hear yet again how great he is.

'Look, mate, I had my own sect. The Black Church of Eternal Hellfire.'

'Of which you were the only member.'

I try to match his left-handed smile for a while before giving up the struggle. 'Not at all. Sasha was in it too. And some rich Americans.'

Shouldn't really have told him that. They might find the bodies from last Easter, and he might get to testify against us, but no matter. He is more interested in talking about himself, as usual.

'Very impressive,' he drawls. 'The Black Order have members on five continents, a wealth of material available on the Internet, books, CDs.'

'Suppositories . . .' chips in Sasha.

'Videos for sale and an ever-growing army of acolytes world-wide. We make the Golden Dawn look like a vicarage tea party. We . . .'

'My gang's bigger than your gang,' I say in a five-year-old's voice.

He tries to clear his chest and sinuses before replying.

'It's simply a statement of fact,' he says eventually. 'I'm sorry if you find it upsetting. Incidentally, novices are allowed to join only if they face an ordeal and triumph over the obstacles we put in front of them.'

'Er, we didn't say we wanted to join.'

'But you want to know who the Dungeonmaster's Apprentice is. I could even introduce you to the Dungeonmaster himself.'

He's hooked Sasha with this one.

'But before you join any magickal sect you have to undergo an ordeal, an initiation ceremony. Don't look like that. You know all this already, dear.'

'Because you've already said it,' I say, relieved that someone else has no memory either.

He gives me his dead hard face and continues regardless. 'And all you've got to do is to drive through Brixton, slowly, in those uniforms.' We know, we know. 'And you have to keep a camcorder record to prove it,' he says. 'It's part of the quest. If you want to progress in the order, you must risk everything.'

'Ooh, it's just like *The Magus*,' I say in a silly northern voice.

'What is your real accent?' says Richard. 'What did you start off with?'

'Suburban Liverpool.'

'A Scouser!' he says, practically jumping up and down with glee.

'Could there be anything worse?' says Alice silkily.

'Birmingham,' I say, but no one can hear me for the popping

of champagne corks, the blowing of party squeakers and a carnival band bursting into some salsa-flavoured dance music. When they have finished doing the opening flurry of piss-poor Scouse accents and footie jokes I manage to ungrit my teeth with some difficulty.

I look at Sasha. She's game, of course. I'm not. I never am, but she is not going to let a little detail like that stand in her way.

She adds a skirt to the rest of her Nazi schoolgirl rig. Brown is the wrong colour for any sort of human clothing, but she manages to carry it off somehow. She gives me a mock curtsy with a lewd, twisted smile while Richard pats me on the shoulder.

'Break a leg,' he says. 'You're going to be sensational, darling.'

The mild mushroom shimmer makes the experience of leaving the house even edgier than it would have been anyway. It's a relief to get into the cab and find the wheel without cracking up.

'Suits you, sir,' says Sasha, from the jump seat, appropriating a catch phrase that had not outstayed its welcome back then.

'I suppose it does,' I say, shying away from the sight of my face after a brief look in the mirror.

'Cheer up,' she says. 'I thought you would really be into this.'

'You know where I really like to be. At home on the couch, taking little homoeopathic sips of evil filtered through books and the telly. I don't like the real thing snuffling and snarling at my knackers.'

For some reason she's happy now. I certainly didn't intend her to be. As a general rule, whenever I'm trying to annoy her it doesn't work and attempts at sweetening her up always have the opposite effect. 'That's *so* sweet,' she says, with sparkly eyes and sweetly puckered dimples in her cheeks. 'You like cocooning with me.'

'If you say so. Look, if we don't get out alive you might as well know . . .'

'I know. You love me. I love you.' She smiles – another real one.

We say a few other things that only we will ever know, then it's time to put the key in the ignition and let a mild diesel fog build up inside the cab.

'You'd never leave me, would you?' she says once we are under way. Which should be my line, really. I'm obviously never going to leave *her*.

'You put yourself down too much,' she says, having read all that from my rueful smile.

'I'm English. It's in the tapwater or something. It's in the exhaust fumes we breathe. It's the chemicals in white bread.'

Her face is saying 'shut up, don't ruin it' so I do. She's filming now anyway, and I never want to say or do anything as soon as a camcorder is involved.

The least troublesome route to Brixton still involves a couple of traffic jams, which doesn't seem fair after midnight, but I pass the time by shifting my packet around inside my rubber knickers and admiring my reflection in the mirror.

At a traffic light near Brixton we are waved down by a young policeman who looks like he needs a clip round the ear and sending home. It's way past his bedtime.

He doesn't look so innocent once he catches sight of Sasha, whom he then favours with a quirky little grin. 'I see,' he says. 'Switch that off, madam.' Sasha complies instantly and sits up straighter, with her legs very close together.

'You do realise I could probably do you under the race relations laws,' he says. 'You might be committing a public order offence.'

'Not us, officer,' I say. 'We are on our way to a party.'

'Well, I hope it's not in Golders Green.' He laughs at his own joke, and I somehow manage to join in as he waves us on.

'What's Golders Green?' says Sasha, as soon as we are crawling towards Brixton Road.

'Big Jewish area.'

'Well, you could drive through there no problem. What are they ever going to do except queue up to get on the trains to the nearest concentration camp?'

'Sasha!' I say, rather wearily, as you might address a naughty child who isn't really going to listen. She puts her tongue out and, well, you have to forgive her. You just do.

Nothing much happens on our slow drive through Brixton because the street people are either too bombed to notice us or all too aware that we are overgrown students playing a prank. The international sign language for wanker crops up more than once and seems to sum us up best.

'You know what we should do?' I say, as I drive back down towards the South Circular, mission accomplished. 'Break into Richard's boat, weigh the body down and tip it over the side. Why doesn't he have an alarm anyway? There's loads of council flats round there.'

'He used to have that dog,' says Sasha. 'And in any case he uses the dagaz rune to protect against intruders. He probably visualises a protective barrier of fire too.'

'Thanks for the tip. I'll watch out for that if I ever break in.'

'That's what those two triangles are drawn above the doors and windows,' she says, never more eager to impart knowledge than when she knows I don't want to hear it. 'You know, the ones placed side by side, tip to tip?'

She smiles as she watches the light dawn on my face as I sort this out.

'You have just invoked the power of the sun; light, peace and prosperity,' she says. 'Just by visualisation.'

'Great. Maybe that will prevent Hugh's spirit crawling up my arsehole. I'd hate to have him possessing me. Not to mention all the other spirits floating around in there.'

Sasha is looking at me rather thoughtfully.

'It's a shame, really,' she says. 'I wouldn't mind stringing you up occasionally.' She smiles impishly to indicate that this is a joke, and I give her a much weaker smile back to indicate that we all like a laugh now and again.

Back at Alice's we have to wait a long time on the doorstep.

'We should kill him just for this,' whispers Sasha, as the seconds tick by.

'I'll get Richard, don't you worry about that,' I say, as Sasha rolls her eyes. 'And I'll settle Alice too.' And Cathy, but I'm not going to say that out loud.

Suddenly inspiration strikes. 'Tell you what, I'll do it right now. Tell him I've gone to get some dope or something. I'll be back soon.'

'What?'

'I'll be back in less than an hour.'

Just then the door opens and the maid awaits Sasha's instructions. From the look that passes between them and the way Sasha waves me off, it would seem that there is no pressing need for me to hurry back.

A call on the mobile determines that Wayne Valentine has the chemicals I need and that he still lives on the same council estate a short drive away. I've known this guy for decades, in which time nothing has happened except that his silly goatee beard has turned white, he has lost a couple of wives and some children, and even fewer people like the brand of jazz that got him into this mess in the first place. He is no better at selling drugs than he is at random faffing about on the trombone, but as there is an insatiable demand for chemical delirium he has managed to survive and even prosper. Once I have the drugs I insist on leaving immediately, and Wayne reminds me that it looks bad to have an endless stream of visitors who only stay for only five minutes. That's what we always say, and I leave hoping never to go back – as I always do.

The drive to Greenwich doesn't take long at this time of the night, and it's easy enough to break into Richard's houseboat. I manage to walk through Richard's protective barrier of imaginary fire without sustaining any third-degree burns, and from there it's a simple matter to deal with his padlocked door. Simple enough if you carry the precision cutting tools I always keep in the cab in case Sasha needs rescuing from any of her bondage clients. Once inside, I remember the dagaz runes painted around the door, but I must have somehow disabled them, too, as the ceiling fails to fall on my head and neither does Thor himself show up with his magic hammer.

I fix up the booby trap that should enable me to permanently remove Richard from our lives or at the very least subject him to a type of radical tissue modification that even he is unlikely to enjoy, then have a quick peek at Hugh to check he's still there. I soon wish I hadn't as Richard has been up to his old tricks again.

We are talking radical body sculpture here, the sort of cutting-edge deconstruction that would make Sasha and Cathy swoon. Hugh is now wearing this season's asymmetrical facial styling. One side is courtesy of his parents and that heartless satirist Mother Nature, but the other has been carved into crisscross bands of muscle and sinew. Glinting teeth and bone make thrilling accessories, and the missing eyeball is certainly innovative.

Lower down we have pleats and tucks, strange exploratory gouges – and there's the eyeball, popped in the navel and . . . sorry, I lost concentration when a small rodent just dived out of a hole in his stomach. Some of the incisions are in the shape of runes, which means that Richard will now consider himself to be at the height of his powers, having invoked his favourite gods and goddesses.

I can't resist carving an M in there. This rune signifies the horse, solar power, and transport from one place to another and also from one mode of existence to another. It's particularly applicable to Hugh and Richard because it was on the gallows that many sacrifices to Thor were made. They even called it the death-horse at one time. There might just be time for Richard to work out that it also means M for Matthew, my original name. It might even be his very last thought before he rides swiftly off on the transport I have arranged for him. Thinking of that is almost enough to make me attempt a rare smile as I wedge the door shut and drive back to Alice's.

Back in the 1930s again, Alice is pouring tea from a silver pot into china cups. There are cucumber sandwiches and several types of cake. The vibe seems half P.G. Wodehouse and half Dennis Wheatley, what with Alice's fake posh accent and Richard's glowering and cursing, but I just want to go home, as usual. As chance would have it Sasha wants to do the opposite of what I want, so eventually I find myself accepting a nice cup of tea.

'You haven't poisoned this as well?' I say to Alice.

'Don't be silly!' she says, handing round cake.

'I know where *you've* been,' says Richard.

For a split second he has me believing in astral projection and that he knows I have just booby-trapped his houseboat. I manage to return his stare somehow, but he knows something is up.

'It's the uniform! I bet you've been up the common for a quick bonk.'

I would never pay for sex, not the human interactive variety anyway, but saying that would have everyone believing the exact opposite, so I remain silent.

'I never heard anyone real say "bonk" or "romp",' says Sasha. 'You don't romp with your lover, do you?'

'Who has lovers?' says Richard. 'What is this? Mills & Boon? You have babes, you have slaves, you have objects of desire. Love is a social construction.'

It's too dangerous for me to say anything in front of Sasha, so I'm happy to drink my tea while Richard blathers on. Having survived the Brixton ordeal, apparently we have now reached the grade of adeptus minor, which has certainly made my day. I'm glad there are no hard feelings about the beating I gave him earlier on. It was for his own good; certainly not my own pleasure. But just as children seem strangely resentful about well-meaning chastisement I would expect him to harbour some ill will. And to want some revenge. And just then I notice for the first time how intricate the pattern on Alice's drawing-room ceiling is. I'm feeling very relaxed, too, but not as mellow as Sasha is. Her head is slumped on her chest and she is starting to snore. It's about forty years too soon for her to fall asleep in company, and I shouldn't really be falling off my chair and trying to crawl to the door either. I'm not going to get there. The carpet is too comfortable, and there is nothing else to focus on but the sound of Richard's triumphant laughter.

16

THE LIGHTBULB HANGING from a bare wire is still there, still burning my eyeballs with its harsh yellow light. This time I'm going to have to stop pretending something terrible has happened and wake up. I soon wish I hadn't. The realisation that I am naked and cuffed to heavy iron rings set in a cold wet stone floor is unsettling, as are the waves of nausea that force me to evacuate the contents of my stomach. The process of tensing every muscle while naked and restrained is initially reminiscent of one of Sasha's Tantric torment sessions, but I can't imagine anyone developing a taste for this. When the final spasm recedes, and the last drop of bile has trickled upwards, my scabby new tattoo comes to life. It feels like a fierce scald now, rather than the gentle ache I had got used to, but there is no time to worry about that or the other sensations competing for my attention.

Something acrid and bitter is burning into my lungs as a gloved hand sets the lightbulb swinging. Through the shifting shadows I can just about make out Sasha's face. She looks worried, which is puzzling. She never used to like me throwing up when it was a regular part of our morning routine, but maybe she's feeling guilty about doing this to me. I don't remember how this particular game started until I see Richard, and the total recall brings on another wave of nausea. Both of my balls fight each other to try to get back into my body first, but they can't shrink enough to get inside where it's safe and warm, just as I can't slip my wrists or ankles through these tight leather cuffs.

Richard is standing inappropriately close. He's also inappropriately naked and inappropriately erect. There are pear-shaped weights hanging off his Prince Albert ring, tilting his penis downwards, and my first thoughts are not whether this affects the Lacanian theory of the penis as signifier of lack-in-being but where he is going to stick that thing.

It's probably superfluous by now to say he is smoking a fat, untidy joint, but what's new is that he laughs as the hot hash chips fall out of the end on to his bare flesh. Once he knows I'm watching he holds the lighted end against his shaven stomach and grins at me while I consider what form his revenge might take.

As this is Richard, there is so much more than mere rape to be considered. He has all sorts of invasive procedures on offer. We are talking access all areas here; by prick, fist and dildo; with catheters, sprockets, tubing – and no doubt much more that only he could ever think of.

Cathy is here too, also skyclad, as the goody-goody witches say, and also cuffed to the heavy iron rings set in the floor. She has been gagged, and there is a large dark wet patch around where she is lying. The air is foul with urine as well as vomit. I can now see the coiled dragons that cover her entire body, but

I'm still no closer to reading what might be inside her head other than that she is alive and unafraid.

Sasha is standing in the space between us holding a bowl. Her wrists and ankles are tied to each other by the same cheap leather cuffs that are keeping Cathy and me at Richard's beck and call. She is still wearing her Nazi schoolgirl stuff, but as she is also wearing a grubby white gag there is not much possibility of an impish smile. She looks pale and frightened as she concentrates very hard on catching drips from a large upside-down bottle placed directly above me. A whirring sound starts up and the nozzle moves very slowly and jerkily over to Cathy. It's some sort of Meccano contraption that looks far too rickety to bear the weight of the bottle, which is something else to worry about. Sasha follows the progress very carefully, catching the drips as she does so.

'The torment of Loki, just in case you were wondering,' says Richard. The bruises I inflicted are a bit bigger now but have yet to colour up. There is no way of knowing how long ago all that happened. 'It's sulphuric acid in the bottle. It may sting a little.'

'The torment of Loki,' I say. 'I don't want to know, but you're going to tell me anyway.'

My voice is higher than it should be, but I am maintaining well. Especially since there's a bundle of rags over in the corner next to a dark red pool of congealed blood. A thin white limb with a burn blotch on it is sticking out of the sackcloth thrown over it. Alice, I suppose, now surplus to Richard's requirements.

'Loki was one of the brightest stars in the northern pantheon but, like Lucifer, he was unwilling to serve. A perfect model for eternal teenagers such as myself. Once he was caught by the giantess Skaldi and tethered underneath a giant serpent which dripped venom. His faithful wife – sorry, Sasha, didn't mean to laugh there – his faithful wife caught the drops in a bowl. It was said that whenever she emptied the bowl and the drops of ice-cold venom landed on him, the earth quaked as he writhed in torment.'

Richard has been prancing around like a prat during this recital, crouching and pulling faces, throwing shapes with his fingers. I wonder if this has anything to do with the 'runic yoga' he once mentioned, which seemed to consist of trying to approximate the shapes of runes with your body while chanting stuff like, and I quote, 'Pu, pa, pi, pe, po'.

It's hard to believe that this is the Teutonic voodoo that launched Hitler on his way, but Richard is adamant that he is channelling the same dark forces. Hence this Nordic history lesson perhaps.

'Loki's destiny is, however, always to break free. Until the seventh of these great escapes. The final escape will initiate doomsday, the death of the gods. So, do you feel lucky, punk?'

I already made one miraculous escape last year. It doesn't seem likely that I will make another, but the important thing to remember is that this could be part of an initiation ordeal. He is not going to kill his own troops. But that doesn't explain that bundle of rags in the corner next to the sticky puddle of blood.

'Is that Alice over there?' I say, looking at the dark shape and the bony burned leg sticking out at an unnatural angle.

'Yes,' he says. 'Just be thankful you're still alive.'

I have mixed feelings about that as Richard steps closer.

'Scared?' he says.

Well, it's not the possible prostate massage with some chap's jade stalk – been there, done that – it's the fluid exchange, with all that might entail.

'HIV-positive?' I say.

'I am above such mundane concerns,' he says, but he does

seem to be hopping about with more energy than before. Maybe he doesn't always believe in magic.

'Aren't you supposed to pay for dinner at least?' I say, in a high, croaky voice.

He's not amused, but the longer I talk the longer it's going to be before he gets down to whatever he's going to do.

'Surely dinner and a movie is the contractual minimum in these circumstances.'

'It's a shame you're too out of it to beg,' he says. 'It's a pity we can't wait till you can feel real fear.'

'Do what you're going to do,' I say. 'I really couldn't care less.'

His face drops when he sees I mean it. Which isn't bravery or anything remotely like it; it's probably what was in the knockout drops.

'You're no fun,' he says with a silly pout.

I suppose what's preventing him from hurting me is that Sasha is holding a large amount of sulphuric acid in that dish. There's no reason why she shouldn't throw it over him. And as my head clears slightly I can see that this may just be the price of admission to the Black Order. Your average cult usually has some sort of death and rebirth process to make you feel different from the mob, the merely human. But that stinking bundle in the corner looks awfully like Alice. And she doesn't look like she's going anywhere ever again. Not of her own volition anyway.

'What's she doing here?' I say, looking at Cathy.

'I told her she could tattoo Hugh's corpse, and she couldn't get here fast enough. She's obsessed by finding a new canvas for her art. Silly cow. Her weakness is art. I wonder what yours is?'

'It's cowardice. I just want to go home.'

The whirring sound starts up and the nozzle drifts back over to me with Sasha very carefully following with her bowl.

'The torment of Loki,' says Richard. 'I always wanted to stage it. But it's not enough for a real artist just to re-create. I wanted to invent something.'

He raises his eyebrows and leaves them raised. I'm supposed to guess what this invention might be. And I would really rather not.

'Very well. Sasha must make a choice between the two of you. When I return she will have made her choice. One of you two will be admitted to the Black Order.'

'And what happens to the other?'

'Oh, I'm sure Skaldi will think of something. She's quite inventive, you know. And cruel. The biggest, meanest queen you'll ever meet.'

Richard blows us all a kiss.

'Funny, that,' I say. 'I was only invoking her last night.'

'And here I am! Who says magic doesn't work?'

'I want my money back.'

'Money?' says Richard.

'Three ten-pound notes stuffed into a stripper's garter.'

'Well, what do you expect? You can't buy a goddess for thirty quid. Now, before I go I want you to wear this mask.'

'It's the same one Hugh was wearing,' I say.

'Yes! Think you'll survive any longer?'

'So you killed him.'

'No!' says Richard. 'He knew the risks. I have never killed anyone. Ever. Unlike you. And her.'

Which was supposed to be our little secret. I look at Sasha, but she's too busy concentrating on catching the drips of sulphuric acid. Maybe I shouldn't try to make her feel too guilty right now. She should concentrate. Her arms must hurt holding the dish upright. It's bound to splash on to my skin anyway as the level in the dish rises. Something else to look forward to.

'How do we know this isn't just one of your pranks?' I say. 'That could just be bleach.'

Sasha is moaning through her gag now and shaking her head. I really shouldn't have said that, I suppose. Richard stomps his foot to show he is annoyed then uses his dagger to carefully flick a very small amount on my skin. Whatever is in the dish stings, then burns and carries on burning. It's like being eaten alive – not that I know what that feels like. My left thigh will never be the same, probably, but it could have been worse. The burn is quite close to where my stock of downloadable DNA is stored.

'You worry too much,' says Richard. 'It's quite a light solution actually. I could have made it far worse for you. Still potentially fatal, of course, but Sasha will keep the drips off your body. Won't you, Sasha?'

She nods her head.

'It used to be fashionable in Victorian times actually. Throwing vitriol in people's faces. You could scar someone for life, rather like those pathetic tattoos of yours.'

'They are not pathetic; they are magnificent.'

'You are messing with the runes and they don't like it. They must be treated with respect.' He is now using an awestruck whisper and stretching his face into the sort of stagy grimaces that Steven Berkoff might consider a little bit overdone.

'The runes,' he says, creeping in and out of the shadows. 'Misuse the runes and you will soon know about it. Himmler thought he could appropriate the Hagall rune for his elite troops, and look what happened on the Russian front.'

'Hagall is the ice rune?'

'It means hail! Some magician you are. But a million lives were lost in the ice. Lost as a result of Himmler's meddling with forces he could not ultimately control.'

It's getting harder to ignore the feeling that he thought the

Second World War was all right really – just a shame about the result.

'You don't find all this Nordic stuff a tad right wing?' I say.

This merits a sneer, no hand-waving or face-pulling. Perhaps he is running out of whatever chemical is cranking him up to this level.

'You must pass beyond the false dichotomy of right and left before you can hope to make any progress as a magician,' he says. 'The adept sees too clearly to be politically correct.'

He smiles as he watches me fumble for a reply, but then inspiration strikes once more.

'It was once customary for those who were too scared to die in battle to carve a rune into their body and then bleed to death – the origin of the expression "red-letter", and also why Sundays and holidays are often printed in red on calendars.'

Can't see the relevance myself. Unless we are back to proving that Richard knows more about everything than everyone else. Which is fine by me.

'Was your father a teacher? Or mummy perhaps?' I say.

Richard closes his eyes briefly before the silly grin returns. It was only a moment, but I had him and he knows it. It's surprising how often you can get the most implacable enemy of society to squirm just by mentioning Mummy and Daddy. I've seen it with all sorts of overgrown children – anarchists, self-styled satanists, transgressive writers called Dennis. Just mention their parents and watch them squirm.

I catch the glint of a camera's eye.

'You filming this, Richard?'

'I would hardly keep a record of a capital crime, now would I? Snuff movies are illegal. You know that.'

Rather than think about what he means I just have to keep

on arguing. 'They don't exist,' I say, quoting Sasha. And she knows. She's spent long enough looking for them.

'Maybe they will after tonight,' says Richard jovially. 'In any case, you are not going to die. If Sasha is careful. I'm nipping out for a while. It's so exciting, isn't it This is art! Real living, breathing art torn from your very soul!'

There's no point in telling Richard he is sick, or a maniac, or even that he never grew up. He already knows.

'Were you abused?' I say, God knows why. Neither of us cares.

'I was not abused!' says Richard, waving his arms around again. 'On the contrary. I enjoyed every minute of it.'

'Your father?'

'Grandfather. I'll show you what he did when I get back. Give you a practical demonstration. Just got to go to the boat to get more drugs. Amazing how you keep running out, isn't it? Remember, Sasha. You have to make a choice.'

With that he fits the mask over my head, and once that's done I can hear my breath and raised pulse rate so much better. This would be the time to plead, but I don't know whether I'm supposed to be shutting up now to conserve oxygen. How long did Hugh last in here: forty-five minutes? It will feel like longer, of course, but the void afterwards will be for ever. A door clangs shut some way in the distance and then there is only the faint sounds of our static world: the whirring of the motor that drives the mechanical arm, fevered breathing, rattling and clanking as we move our cuffs.

There is now time only to make the usual futile promises. If we get out of this we will never do this again. Which is what we always say. But it's still profoundly true. Until I get out of these shackles, when I'm likely to be surprisingly similar to the way I always used to be.

If we get out.

If my booby trap works Richard won't be coming back, and we will be stuck here until what's in the bottle runs out. Only then will Sasha be able to move, but she still won't have a key to the padlocks or a sharp knife. I will suffocate, making Sasha's choice between me and Cathy a great deal easier. Before that, Richard may well come back with an adequate supply of coke to make the process of torturing us just that little bit more interesting.

Sasha's familiar perfume and the sort of noxious sweat she would never normally allow to accumulate is now close enough to compete with the smell of the rubber mask as the most intense pain I have ever felt burns through my right wrist. When I've stopped cursing I realise that there is more play in the cuffs.

Well, you can't make an omelette without breaking eggs, as Sasha always says, and it wasn't possible to drip acid on the cuffs without spilling a little of that stuff. Hurts, though. And has probably messed up the tattoo on my right wrist. She's going to have to burn the other cuff off, and that is really close to the scalding pain of the new tattoo.

Agonising minutes pass while she very carefully drips minute amounts of acid on to the cuffs in the seconds between when the bottle is over my body and when it is above Cathy. I use the time to promise myself a nervous breakdown when I get out of here.

After a number of goes with the dish it's possible to rip through the thin leather, but that still leaves the other cuff. Every now and again a minute spill gets my wrist.

'Use the pain,' she whispers. 'Concentrate! Picture Richard and what you're going to do to him.'

Instead I picture Cathy's face and watch it crumble as the burning continues. Sasha is more careful now as she judges how few drops of acid will burn the leather, but it hurts and goes on hurting long enough for me to add an extra little request from whichever malevolent demon might be listening that Richard should get back here intact. My little booby trap is too good for him. I want him here, now I have two functioning hands.

I rip the mask off and tell Sasha to crouch so that I can remove the gag. Perhaps five more awkward sweaty minutes and she manages to burn off the leg cuffs without too much agony for me. As soon as I feel able I go over and smash Richard's camera to pieces to take my mind off the pain. During a lull in the frenzy I can hear Sasha moaning through the gag. Of course, how selfish of me. I undo it slowly and carefully as she is still protecting Cathy's body from the drips of acid.

'What did you do that for?' she says, utterly outraged. 'I really wanted to see that film.'

Of course, I was forgetting that we were creating a work of art.

'Sorry,' I say, which seems to be the quickest way out of that. Besides, I'm sure I wasn't lit right. And fear of a painful death does terrible things to a man's endowment. I certainly don't want that preserved for posterity.

'Your skin's going to be sore,' she says, and the concern in her voice warms every cell in my body.

'I'm going to need your famous healing powers,' I say.

For an instant it looks like that acid is going in my face. The subject of her healing hands has been recently judged unfit for humour, probably because her last attempt at shamanic healing left her trembling in bed for three straight days. She said it was because the lizard-god form she assumed to remove Poodle Patty's thrush proved impervious to banishment. Some sceptics, myself among them, were of the opinion that fasting, sleep deprivation and mouldy magic mushrooms can cloud the diagnostic faculties. In the course of a long discussion during which

I sustained a minor flesh wound we eventually agreed not to discuss it.

'I'll get something to cut Cathy loose,' I say, and then wonder if that's possible as I lurch off into the darkness. I pause by the dark reeking bundle that used to be Alice, but I don't want to see the state Richard has left her in. Immediately outside what looks to be the cellar of some private house are our clothes. The money and keys are still there, and even my magic shiny red boots are unscathed. A quick scout up the stairs takes me into a garage in which one of Alice's stupid old cars is parked. Vintage-car enthusiasts will insist on knowing that it's a green one. More important, to her, is that it's British, from a time when we ruled the world. Further investigation reveals that this is Alice's house, but I don't want to explore any further alone. I find a sturdy pair of scissors in a toolbox and return to cut Cathy loose.

'Water,' she is saying, as soon as I have removed the gag.

'Don't cut her free just yet,' says Sasha.

'What?'

I had thought we were on the last lap. I can almost see my *Hound of the Baskervilles* coffee cup with the red moon that turns white in response to the hot liquid. I can almost taste the freshly ground high-roast Colombian blend inside it. If I close my eyes I can almost see our couch. But Sasha seems to have a score to settle.

'I want some answers,' she says, and the tone of voice is ominous.

I suddenly realise I'm crouching between Sasha and Cathy. And the bowl of sulphuric acid.

'Yesterday you were quite happy to shag her. What's the problem now?'

'I want to know why she can just walk into our life, wreck it and then walk out again.'

I look at Cathy's blank face and dead eyes. Whatever's in there is permanently off limits to the likes of me.

'Can't you just get a cat next time?' I ask Sasha. 'If you want to be used and then ignored by some beautiful animal?'

I have polished and rehearsed that for days. In my version Sasha runs over and begs for forgiveness, but as usual Sasha has forgotten her lines. She is more concerned with glaring at Cathy. I haven't a clue where all this came from unless it's love. Sasha is theoretically past all that, but you never know. There is not much she doesn't rule out. She wouldn't like the comparison, but her ethics are like a fat American's elastic-waist jeans, built roomy enough to accommodate just about anything. But falling in love for real? There are limits. After I have cut Cathy free from the wrist cuffs she bats my hands away and does the rest herself.

'You're welcome,' I say. She looks right through me. I wish she hadn't written all over me now. Even if I get it covered up, there will always be a little bit of her inside me. It's almost enough to make me reach for the sulphuric acid to burn it off.

'I want a cigarette,' says Sasha as Cathy goes in search of her clothes.

'You don't smoke.'

'Can't I have one now?' she says, as if I could stop her anyway. 'Alice will have some.'

Before Sasha can rifle a corpse's pockets in search of an admittedly deserved and possibly therapeutic cigarette, Cathy is back, bedraggled but looking better for having her clothes on again.

'I'm going,' she says. 'This is out of control. You will never see me again.'

It's not often Sasha has nothing to say, but she has no answer to this. Perhaps it's just the flat mechanical voice that has crushed her. The way Cathy is speaking, it is obvious she feels no affection for Sasha, certainly none of that messy made-up stuff some people call love. Sasha moves closer to her. I really hope she is not going to humiliate herself by pleading with her. But it turns out that she needs to be that close to spit accurately into her face.

Cathy lets it happen, wipes it off then turns and walks slowly out of the door. Sasha is on the brink of tears. She has done the worst thing she could think of and it still didn't matter, didn't even ripple the surface of the pond. This isn't a good time for me to say anything, but I have to get her moving out of there somehow.

'She was just a tourist,' I say. 'You were part of her London experience. You'll get over it.'

Sasha turns her crumpled face on me, sees that she looks weak, remembers that's not supposed to happen, then recovers quickly. She still has to blow her nose, though, and there's no cool or stylish way of doing that.

'I suppose you're right,' she says, so quietly you can barely hear it. 'She was the best Top I ever had, though.' 'Female,' she adds, but it's too late by then.

'I never liked American jargon,' I say, setting myself up for a long rant, but Sasha nips into a pause for breath.

'It's not jargon. Top and Bottom is non-judgemental.'

Well, at least if she can be bothered to bicker she must be back to normal again.

'What's judgemental about submissive and dominant?' I say, gently herding her to the door.

'It implies subservience when, as you know, submissives whine so much that they are actually in charge. Also Tops often yearn for their slaves when a relationship has ended.'

She looks rather pointedly at me, and I narrow my eyes because I am not going to discuss my one-time slave, a little astral terrorist who just cannot be exorcised. It's not the real person inside my head – just the ghost I created – but she's certainly got staying power. I'll say that for her.

'We have got to get out of here,' I say.

But Sasha isn't interested in that. She is backing away from me with her face crumpling into tears once more, her mouth wide open. She starts to scream, and when I turn round I see why.

17

THE BUNDLE OF rags that was Alice is moving. Slowly and unsteadily, a trembling white arm burrows through the sackcloth and reveals a zombified version of the Alice we knew and loved. Her face is now even whiter than it was before, perhaps accentuated by the thick crust of blood around her puffed-up lips. She doesn't look well.

The first sign that her reasoning processes are unaffected comes when she reaches inside her cardie for a crushed pack of cigarettes and lights one up. Ripples of joy spread slowly through her as she has a feline little stretch and purr before losing it to a major coughing fit. Eventually the seismic tides inside her lungs calm down enough for me to ask what happened. Rather than answer, she continues smoking in an aloof manner, something she's rather good at.

'We thought you were dead,' says Sasha, her tone of voice implying that her recovery is a mixed blessing.

'I'm still here,' says Alice. 'He hits harder than Matt does, though.'

I pretend I don't know what she's talking about while Sasha stares at the two of us.

'Not hard enough, though,' I say. 'You're still alive.'

'You going to tell me what it is with you two?' says Sasha. 'Did you fuck her or something? Why is that such a dark secret?'

I look over at Alice.

'Do you want to tell her?' I say, past caring now.

Alice stubs her cigarette and wheezes for a while. I'm expecting her to gloat now that she can ruin the rest of my life, but she just looks very tired. For a tantalising moment we don't know whether she is going to light up a cigarette right away or whether she will wait another ten seconds or so. As soon as she's fired up another fag, and the sputum has been dredged up and swallowed again, she starts to croak her way through the explanation.

'I was still a man at the time, darling,' she says. 'Back then. Twenty years ago. I let Matt here stick his pride and joy inside me. Right up the arse. He fucked me, grunted for a bit but didn't come. Then he fell asleep. The usual drunken performance. Because he was such a macho man at the time he gave me a black eye. When he found out I was a man.'

I look down at the fourth finger of my right hand which is still bent out of shape.

'That's what you were ashamed of?' says Sasha, to me.

It's hardly enough to make the average priest or MP blush. Sasha even sounds disappointed. With any luck Alice will leave it at that. But I never have any luck.

'I was so naive in those days,' she continues. 'And I loved him so much. He just took whatever I could give him. A roof whenever he couldn't crawl home. Food, drink, drugs. And then he took two thousand pounds off me to remove a curse. I was always too ashamed to tell anyone. I wrote it off.'

Sasha looks at me for a long moment. 'Matt would boast about something like that,' she says. 'There must be something else.'

Alice's humourless smile tightens, setting off waves of wrinkles. Maybe she won't tell after all.

'Come on,' says Sasha. 'Or is it just those bacon sandwiches he eats when he thinks I'm not looking? He's frightened of something. There's another secret.'

'I was forgetting,' says Alice. 'You are one of these weaklings who venerates animals. Maybe even one of those occultnik dabblers who thinks that cats are a manifestation of the Goddess. Or something you can project yourself into. Or the symbol of the Egyptian Goddess Bast, the spirit of sexuality. How absurdly sentimental. He must be scared that I would tell you about our little cat sacrifice.'

I put my head in my hands. I can't look at Sasha. This really could be the end now. I was never sure if it had actually happened, being ripped to the tits at the time, but this is the worst possible moment to find out. There is no point in pretending I wasn't there, but I'm still pretty sure I didn't do it.

'You killed a cat,' says Sasha. And by the look on her face I may be in for some non-consensual s/m in the near future. Something that is likely to push me past my limits right into the red zone. And so safe words will save me now.

'I didn't kill it,' I say. 'But I didn't stop her doing it. Look, I was a drunken nineteen-year-old moron . . .'

Suddenly her face is back in neutral. She turns to Alice. 'It was you who put the skinned cat on our door, wasn't it?'

'It was dead already, my dear. Richard had a little accident while trying to invoke something or other. I thought I might as well get some use out of it so I paid one of the novices to do it.

Come on, don't look like that. I could have told Jason Skinner's family where you are. I know Matt killed his brother,' she says. 'At least give me credit for keeping that a secret.'

Sasha looks over at me, but I can't tell what she wants me to say or do. I'm still surprised to get off so lightly from the cat sacrifice. If I have got off, that is.

'I was expecting you to be annoyed,' I say.

'What's done is done,' says Sasha. 'You're not that person now. Even then you were just a silly little boy. Did the cat scratch you?'

'No,' says Alice. 'We were quick and humane.'

'Then so must I be,' says Sasha, and quickly pulls her Stanley knife out. There's just time to watch it gleam and think about how the metal contrasts with her silver rings before she draws the sharpened blade across Alice's face. She screams then puts her scrawny burned hand up to her face. I can't help thinking that Alice should stay still rather than increase her pulse rate by shaking her head from side to side, but it turns out that Sasha was just rubbing the flat side of the blade across her face. There is no incision and no blood; just another one of Sasha's little games. It's enough to make Alice burst into tears, though, an ugly sight and sound. Sasha looks very still, very centred, as Alice seems to shrink and age before our eyes.

'Please . . .' says Alice, but one look at my little tigress's face and it's clear that there is no point in asking for mercy. Sasha orders Alice to strip. Alice whimpers something to the effect that she won't undress completely, which is fine by me, but Sasha is insisting.

'Do it!' she says, brandishing the knife.

'I won't! You can cut me to pieces.'

'OK,' says Sasha, waving the knife again, which triggers more tears.

All this grief is starting to get to me now. I haven't got the nerves to listen to that. She will have to be gagged. While I'm looking for tape or a stocking we can stuff in her mouth, Alice tries to crawl past us, sobbing as she does. That's almost moving, but Sasha just yanks her back then gives her a few with her shiny silver boots.

'Hold her down,' says Sasha, very quietly.

I am in no position to argue. Someone has to pay for the sacrificed cat, and it's not going to be me. I notice that Alice's flesh is very cold to the touch. As it always has been.

'Shut her up,' says Sasha, as Alice starts howling again.

'You can't kill her,' I say, but it comes out like a question.

Sasha's lips are pressed very tightly together, and her pinprick pupils and furrowed brow seem to be saying, 'Oh, yes, I can.' She opens her silver cigarette case which contains her syringes and gear and proceeds to prepare a shot of . . . what precisely?

'I thought all the coke had gone,' I say.

'Richard loves giving me drugs,' she says. 'He knows you can't afford to. He wants me to be his superior slave too.' She laughs at the look on my face then shakes her head, pleased that she can still pull the rug out from under me.

'First we should get rid of Alice, though,' she says, holding the syringe up to the light. 'A nice convenient overdose. Don't like needles, do we, dear? Never mind.'

I'm still holding Alice down while she sobs and begs for mercy, but Sasha just flexes a wrist then shoots herself up instead. Her eyes glint at me while I stand there feeling rather foolish.

'I really thought you were going to do it,' I say.

'It's *real* hard fooling you,' she says.

I will have my revenge for that remark. One day. When I have thought of something sufficiently waspish. Although by that time Sasha may well be wheeling me around and spoonfeeding me with easily digestible soup. But for the moment I'm standing here in the headlights of Sasha's beaming smile.

'What shall we do about Richard?' I ask. She can't be bothered with that till I say, 'What would Emma Peel do?'

'The first thing she would do is change into some tight leather,' says Sasha, all excited now as she turns to Alice. 'Have you got a catsuit?'

Alice turns away in contempt. She despises anything to do with modern fabrics, comic books, television or indeed anything that would confuse a nice gel born before the war.

'Come on!' says Sasha. 'You must have some fancy dress.'

'It is not "fancy dress",' begins Alice before she realises she's too ill for all that. Instead, she leads us to her robing-room, where Sasha finds some leather trousers and a jacket.

'Look! An eye patch!' says Sasha. She throws it to me. 'Put it on! The left eye!'

She's practically jumping up and down now. 'Odin was blinded in one eye, a symbol of his occult powers, his power over the dark, hidden realms of the unconscious. By wearing it you will invoke Odin.'

It's best not to argue; it only encourages her. Instead, I put it on and look in the mirror, dreading the results. To people unschooled in northern mysticism, eye patches signify only some old berk trying to look like pirate at a fancy-dress party, but at least there is only one red-rimmed bloodshot eye on display now.

'Didn't Odin die in Ragnarök?' I say, positive as ever. 'The final conflict between good and evil?'

Sasha doesn't want to hear it.

'Odin is still with us,' she says, giving my uniform a tweak and brushing non-existent fluff off the shoulder. 'And so are you. Let's go and give Richard a taste of his own medicine.'

Once we are all in the cab and driving north I punch his

number into the mobile. Soon I am listening to the supposedly ironic pervy voice with which he always answers the phone.

'Ye-e-es?' he says.

'We got out. Do we win a prize?'

'Well done! Where are you all?'

'In the cab. Where are you?'

'Business to attend to. I knew you would get out somehow or other.'

'Really? We can meet you at the houseboat. Fancy it?'

'But of course, my boy. Such ingenuity deserves a very special reward. How's Alice?'

'Bit of a headache, but she's all right. Look, the battery's going. See you there in half an hour?'

As soon as he says yes I break the connection.

18

'I WONDER IF he's really coming,' says Sasha.

We are parked near the *Cutty Sark*, from where we can see the twists and turns of the river westwards and Christopher Wren's Naval College to our right, near where Richard's houseboat is moored. It's seven in the morning, but I don't feel tired. There's nothing quite so invigorating as a sulphuric acid body splash. Sasha is chiding me for leaving the engine running, as if our shagged-out old planet will notice five more minutes' worth of exhaust fumes. The problem is that these old taxicabs don't always start in a hurry, and we might well need a quick getaway if my little party trick doesn't work.

Not that there aren't other alternative options that would be so much more appropriate, as Sasha just has to remind me. At length. We are now into the second hour of how much better it would have been if she had organised Richard's death. With additional dialogue by Alice, who also would have done it much better.

'It's a shame Cathy was such a bitch,' Sasha is saying. 'I'd love to have done a real *Avengers'* number with her. Lots of fancy dress then the *coup de grâce* with a bow and arrow. Or a crossbow or poison darts or . . .'

'Some pathetic comedy duel with celery sticks,' I say. 'And a cameo role for some resting thespians. A vague hint of prehistoric fem-dom action in ill-fitting leather to get the commuters all steamed up. What wild times the 1960s were . . .'

'Well, you should know.'

'I was at school, you little . . .'

'Children!' croaks Alice.

We both have a sulk and then the bright ideas start to flow once more.

'Why don't we get some enormous animal to fuck him to death?' I say.

'That would be cruel!' says Sasha, genuinely annoyed that I would think of using an innocent animal for such a nefarious purpose.

'But fair,' says Alice, quietly. 'And sometimes the dog's dick gets stuck inside. Try explaining that at Casualty.'

'How do you know that, Alice?' I say. 'Oh, don't tell me.'

'Oh, no!' says Alice, frantically scrabbling in her bag. She has run out of cigarettes, forcing her to scurry to the nearest shop for more supplies.

'What time's Richard due?' says Sasha.

'Must be soon,' I say.

'Will we hear him scream?' says Sasha.

'You bloodthirsty little ghoul,' I say, and back it up with a kiss. My lips are dry, though, and her skin feels ice-cold. It really isn't the moment for romance.

'Even if you do kill him it won't be the end,' says Sasha. 'He'll get us next time.'

Either it's way past her bedtime or she is serious. It's time to invent something uplifting. Anything.

'Well, I hope you are still around,' I say. 'Next time.'

'Wow! Kiss me!' she says. 'Really concentrate on that!'

During the kiss the only thing I am conscious of is how cold her hands are and the way they seem to be pressing too hard against my neck in what some would call a stranglehold.

'It's really winter now, isn't it?' she says, when we come up for air.

'It's certainly gone very cold,' I say, trying to make her feel responsible. 'We should really pack our bags and get out before Cathy or Alice can put us in the dock at the Old Bailey.'

'I know. We can be the other side of the English Channel in a few hours. Open up a new dungeon.'

'With me vetting the sodding clients as usual. The Dungeon-mistress's Apprentice . . .'

'You could be Master Matt again. Take some of that aggression out on the clients.'

I shake my head, thinking of the few times I stood in for her as a slavemaster. It's harder than it looks, you know. And it's always about the clients, the selfish little bleeders. They don't really care about their superiors however much they pretend they do. Still, it's a living, I suppose.

'What have you done anyway?' says Sasha.

'I've set him a booby trap.'

'Richard's no booby. What if it doesn't work?'

'It will work. Look, if it does work . . .'

I'm too scared to say the next bit right away. Which is silly, considering what we have just been through. Sasha is staring at me, and there's no going back so . . .

'If this thing with Richard works, shall we give this open marriage thing a rest for a while? No more Cathy or whoever.'

Now I'm staring at the floor. I'm scared of the reply.

'All right,' she says.

I look at her to see if she means it and it seems to be so. As far as I would ever know.

'*If* it works,' she says. 'All right, I mean it! Don't look at me like that. What is it, anyway? Come on! Don't tease me!'

'Not what you usually say.'

'I mean it!'

'You keep telling me that mysteries cannot be revealed, that they must be experienced by the seeker. He or she must work towards their eventual goal.'

'You've poisoned him!'

I shake my head. 'Guess again.'

'Oh, my God! There he is!'

And so it is. Dead man walking, as they say in Sasha's native land. And with any luck the condemned man has eaten a hearty meal, for these should be the last steps he will ever take. And then I can spend the next five decades or so playing mini-golf or feeding tropical fish. We can't keep getting away with murder, whatever Sasha may think.

Alice climbs back in and torches a fresh cigarette.

'He's got a new dog,' says Sasha. Oh, dear. She really isn't going to like this.

'The dog isn't going to get hurt, is it?' she says, pulling at my sleeve. I'm now looking into the sort of eyes that a small unwanted hound might train on the municipal exterminator shortly after Christmas: big, imploring and utterly guilt-inducing. I had forgotten that in her world the fifty million people who died in the Second World War are the equivalent of one puppy with a thorn in its paw.

The animal in question looks vicious; too large, too many

teeth. We would all be better without its particular contribution to the great debate, but you can't tell Sasha that.

'How could I know he would get another dog? Look at it this way. I'm probably going to save it from a life of brutal sodomy and forced drug abuse.'

'Sounds like the sort of holiday we should be having as soon as this is over,' she says.

While I'm thinking of all the possible ramifications of that, Richard sees that he has been broken into and starts to shout at his dog, which is now barking at the top of its lungs.

'It's probably not going to work,' I say. 'He's probably realised that something's wrong. He may even have nothing to smoke . . .'

An explosion tears the boat apart, leaving a shattered hulk that soon gives up the uneven struggle to stay afloat even before the shower of paper, wood and other debris flutters down to join the other floating rubbish on the surface of the Thames. Somewhere in that lot is six and a half feet's worth of redistributed Richard. And his dog. And the mortal remains of Hugh, of course. It's just a shame I couldn't have lured Cathy aboard, but you can't have everything.

Actually, the explosion doesn't happen, even though I willed it, I visualised it and I practically yanked my right nipple-ring through the flesh while invoking the god of pointless destruction and death – or Mother Nature, as she is more usually known.

'You left the gas on,' says Sasha. 'You remembered he had no sense of smell and hoped he would light a joint. And it didn't work.'

Alice cackles like the malevolent old crone she soon will be while I grip the steering wheel as tightly as I would like to grip her neck. Sasha is saying something I can't quite hear because of blood rushing through my ears and Alice coughing and spluttering her way into a new cigarette.

'Don't worry. I've still got a few tricks up my sleeve,' I say.

The women roll their eyes and sigh, but there's no point in dwelling on that. It's time to say goodbye to Richard, once and for all.

19

'I'VE BROUGHT SOME friends to play,' I say to Richard, once we have joined him and his hound on board the houseboat. He is drawing deeply on a fat, untidy joint while thumping his chest to help clear a path for the smoke.

'Like the eyepatch, dear,' he tells me, then starts off another heroic round of coughing. Some irritating moments later, after what looks like lung tissue has been expectorated, he eventually grins at Alice. 'Aspirin?'

'You bastard,' she says. She looks like she might spit in his face but settles for glowering furiously through the smoke from her cigarette.

'What did you do to her?' I ask Richard, who has tears in his bloodshot eyes as he starts to cough again.

'What did *I* do? I like that. One of her restraint harnesses broke and she dropped on her head. Nothing to do with me, squire.'

Alice is spluttering with rage but deals with it by drawing

harder on her cigarette and exhaling grimly. Her eyes glow like the tip of her cigarette and I almost start to feel scared for Richard. He's not remotely bothered, of course.

'Shoddy workmanship, that's what that was,' he says. 'What about my boat? Someone's broken in.'

'Get rid of the corpse!' I say, a touch on the frantic side. Everyone looks at me and I remember that it's considered de rigeur in this company to simulate indifference to the prospect of a twenty year incarceration with the scum of the earth.

'You worry too much,' says Richard, serious for once as he rolls Hugh's mortal remains inside a carpet and stashes him back in his little cubby-hole. The air is not noticeably fresher as a result of this although home-grown skunk covers a multitude of sins.

Richard remembers his manners. 'Tea?' he asks.

'Have you got coffee?' begins Sasha while Alice stubs one cigarette and lights another one up. I sit down at the table, head in hands, while they blather on about high roast Columbian and hazelnut syrup.

They argue about differing methods of grinding coffee while I grind my teeth until I remember that there is one positive aspect of Richard surviving my ham-fisted attempt at blowing him up. He can tell us who the Dungeonmaster's Apprentice is and then Sasha can let me go back to doing what I'm good at – throwing temper tantrums because I can't find the remote control again.

'Richard!' I say, loudly enough to shut them all up. 'You're supposed to tell us who the Dungeonmaster's Apprentice is. That's the point of all this. Remember?'

Richard smiles broadly as I sit there hating him with every fibre of my being. 'Ooh, I couldn't possibly tell you that!' he says. 'He's much too frightening.'

Sasha moans and fidgets like a child who is about to say 'It's not *fair!*'

Richard smiles fondly and decides to take pity on her. 'Well . . . all right then,' he says. 'We'll have another round of the Porno Olympics. We never got to hear from Matt or Sasha. Tell you what, read me something erotic and I'll tell you who the Dungeonmaster's Apprentice is.'

'I threw mine away,' I say.

'So make something up.'

'Go on, Matt. I could do some of my poetry,' says Sasha. 'It'll be fun.'

We quibble for a bit about the definition of fun – whether it encompasses restraint scenarios involving sulphuric acid for instance – and when I inevitably lose that argument it's time to begin.

Richard is looking very smug for a man facing death by poetry. I could probably survive Sasha's entry but Richard, being a serious poet, might very well take his own life once she gets going. We all scribble away for a few minutes while Richard says about six different things which each deserve a chinning.

'Right,' says Richard, who has put himself in charge as usual. 'Let's hear it, then.'

For once Sasha lets me go first. Probably because I don't want to. 'I've got a homage to the Marquis de Sade,' I say. 'In particular the *120 Days of Sodom*. It seems appropriate while you're here.'

Richard smiles, taking this as a compliment.

'He was another overgrown toddler obsessed with his own arsehole and its contents,' says Sasha, which soon wipes the smile off Richard's face. 'Although you've topped him in one respect,' she continues. 'He didn't go as far as to fashion his own shit into poetry and read it in public.'

Richard's grin is soon back in place. 'Let's hear from the

master,' he says, nodding at me. I pause before reading from my pathetic parody of *120 Days of Sodom*. It's hard to concentrate knowing that Hugh's gun is taped under the table but I really don't know if I've got the balls – or the skill – to rip it from its position, then use it. Probably better to forget about that and just read this dross out.

'The silver-haired libertine reads his own poetry while his helpless listeners writhe and moan in agony. As a stream of fatuous verse pours forth from his spittle-flecked lips the audience cries out for mercy but are offered none.' I look up to check that Richard is not missing the heavy handed reference to himself. He is still smiling, remarkably unscathed. 'Finally they rise and tear him apart, plunging their inflamed members into his torn and bloody flesh. He dies in agony, mourned by no one.'

Richard claps slowly and ironically, then says, 'The elite have to get used to jealous sniping from the underlings. But, just as I need servants,' he pauses to glance round the table, 'You lot need to respond to orders. You should just accept that some are born to rule and others are born to obey.'

Richard gives us all the same sardonic smile, one by one. He wants to see how his underlings are coping with having their noses rubbed in it. And our attempts at concealing our anger just make him laugh even louder. Only Alice seems unconcerned as she rummages in her bag for something.

'But you have to obey the Dungeonmaster's Apprentice,' I say. No doubt just setting myself up for another kicking.

'In a sense,' says Richard. 'But the survival of Nordic culture and the Aryan Race are much more important than my individual ego. Sometimes sacrifices have to be made. Besides, if all goes well, soon he will be working for me. And I will control the pact, I will be the lord of those who imagine themselves to be the cutting edge of contemporary sorcery.'

'It's being middle-aged, isn't it? That's what you can't stand,' says Sasha. 'The loss of your youth. The onset of age. Intimations of mortality.'

There is a touch more ice in Richard's voice as he replies. 'My rivals have tried to kill me,' he says. 'They never succeed. Besides, I have taken the precaution of sacrificing enough underlings to become a God. Even in death, I cannot be defeated. When I shed this skin I will just acquire another.'

'That's handy,' I say.

He shrugs. 'You are content to serve. Or, even more contemptibly, to whinge on about your destiny while doing nothing to change it.'

'Maybe if I had inherited enough money I would also have delusions of grandeur.' My voice is choked by decades of envy and bitterness. And probably by the knowledge that I have the means to change everything close at hand and no excuse not to use it. Bullets could really speak louder than words if I just had the courage to rip the gun from under the table and use it.

'My power is no delusion,' says Richard. He slowly unfurls a hand until it is at shoulder height. 'Even if it is a fiction I never lack for an audience.' Suddenly his fist is bunched and a finger is pointing straight at me. 'But you are content to hide behind a powerful woman. Be thankful she likes lame dogs.'

Sasha is looking at me now. There is no mistaking the message she is sending me; this slight must be avenged. But until he turns his back on me I've got to sit here eating shit and, what's more, Richard has got plenty more of that stuff to shovel onto my plate.

'Did you honestly think you were a worthy opponent for *me*?' he asks, twirling and pirouetting on his seat. Soon he will be up and dancing.

'So you've won,' I say. 'Surely minor deities like yourself should have better things to do than gloat about it.'

'Not really. Absorbing the energy of inferior life forms to boost my own has always been of paramount significance. You, Matt, are just the latest in a long line of useful idiots.' He puts a lot of contempt into those last two words and the little preening fit that comes afterwards. I am willing my heart to stop beating so fast but it's not listening. When I open my mouth to speak I can only manage a few grunts because anger had flooded every cell in my body. And knowing that Sasha is watching this happen just makes it worse. How can our relationship ever survive this total and utter humiliation? He isn't even finished with us yet.

'Only the weak are gracious in defeat,' says Richard. 'I honestly expected more from you three, even if you are unfit to join me on the path of the strong. Oh well, at least it gives me an even greater choice of vanquished enemies to offer up to the Gods.'

'Is that all we are to you?' says Alice. 'Was I also just another potential sacrifice? After all I've done for you?'

Her voice is cracking, there is heartfelt emotion and the pain of betrayal showing on her face. She is making the mistake of courting sympathy and it just triggers another epic sneer from Richard. When he's finished using his height, aristocratic cheek-bones and superior intellect to crush Alice he turns to grin at me. I give him his look back but he's still winning. Once he has established that to his satisfaction, and everyone else's annoyance, he gets his smoking tackle out and starts to skin up.

It shouldn't be a surprise to anyone by now that I am essentially a coward. I am not a member of the master race or one of those pointlessly confident natural leaders that human beings genuflect so readily to. But if Richard turns that look on me once more I'm going to rip this gun from under the table and pull the trigger. I will. Honest. Just you wait and see.

But the shot would be heard by tourists queuing up for their river cruises, Greenwich residents out for a stroll and anyone in the nearby council flats who hasn't got their televisions on at deafening volume to try and cover the noise of their dogs and children. Suddenly I have Sasha's clear, logical voice inside my head telling me that most people don't know what a gun shot sounds like. Most people would put the noise down to something else. She may be right.

There is no way round this. I really have to pull the trigger.

Perhaps if I just frightened him . . .

Richard sees my impotent inwardly-directed rage and starts to laugh again. It soon becomes debatable whether he could stop if he wanted to. I amuse him so much his shoulders are shaking and tears start to leak from underneath his tightly screwed eyes. I look over at Sasha and see from her drooping shoulders and forlorn face that something will have to be done. I reach under the table and slowly detach the tape, almost dropping the gun in the process while Richard just keeps on cackling. That sound is getting more and more annoying but I still manage to click the safety off and bring the gun up above the table but as I do so there is a strong smell of bleach. I make the mistake of turning to look at Alice and as I do so I see that she has extended a perfume bottle halfway across the table.

In the instant I wonder whether that stuff is sulphuric acid and whether it is destined for my face Richard reaches over and tries to grab the gun. But before he can get much further with that Alice has thrown the contents of the bottle into Richard's face. It's a direct hit. For once, he's not smiling. He screams briefly as his hands cover his eyes while Alice watches him very carefully, savouring the moment.

He's soon out of his seat and dancing but this one is never going to catch on. He's bobbing and weaving in a half crouch, hands clutching at his eyes while wheezing and gasping. Any joy I might have felt at this turn of events is mitigated by the knowledge that Alice has ruined my moment. My chance to shine has now been put on permanent hold – again.

Richard croaks on like a frog with laryngitis as the acid eats into his vocal chords. He extends his hands while he tries to find the sink, walking into various painfully protuberant objects as he does so. It's probably too late for water to make any difference to anything but he's game, I'll give him that. Alice puts the empty bottle down on the table and lights a cigarette.

'Someone had to do something,' she says. 'There was no point waiting for *you* to do anything.'

This barb was addressed at me but I'm too busy checking that the gun is loaded to reply. Sasha is looking at me with a puzzled expression, perhaps surprised that I managed to stash a useful weapon somewhere it could have come in handy. While Richard hops around like a cat on a hot tin roof I realise that we are probably not going to find out anymore about the Dungeonmaster's Apprentice. Not from Richard anyway. Alice has finally succeeded where we all failed; she has actually managed to shut him up.

'What did you do that for?' I say. 'I thought you were on his side. Keeping the world safe for the Nordic Race.'

'He has become degenerate,' she said. 'No real magician can afford to become addicted to drugs or his appetite for killing. The taking of a life must be a magickal act. Human sacrifice must only be indulged in when one has a clear purpose. It must never become a cheap thrill.'

'I'll remember that,' I say.

Alice's eyes smoulder briefly in my direction. Then we all go back to pretending to be cool and unconcerned as our guts heave at the horrid noises Richard is making. By the way he is hopping about aimlessly it appears that he has forgotten the all important incantations to ensure appropriate status in the next life. I'm not at all sure he doesn't even say 'Christ!' at one point. Yet another lapsed Catholic I'll be bound.

It's high time someone administered the last rites but all I can come up with is 'Fuck you, Richard.' I intone that many times while we watch the skin on his face dissolve. When he opens his eyes briefly the whites look like badly poached eggs slathered in thin runny ketchup. He's not looking chipper but it is not yet time to cancel the milk and the *Daily Telegraph*, even if he is undoubtedly what my mother would describe as 'very poorly.'

He is still propelling air through his torn throat but it's not really speech any more. The sound he is making is almost enough to elicit sympathy but this is a tough audience. He's going to have to do better than just flailing his arms around, moaning piteously and banging his head on the wall.

'That's starting to get on my nerves,' says Alice. 'Shoot him. Or are you too scared?' 'It's a pointless risk,' I say. 'What if someone hears?'

It's surprising how much glacial contempt Alice can squeeze into one glance. She then stubs her cigarette decisively before walking over to Richard.

'He was going to ensure his immortality by killing us all,' she said. 'The sacrifice of vanquished enemies being one of the oldest magical ceremonies there is. But he didn't predict that I was going to usurp him. Only the truly strong can serve the Dungeonmaster.'

She stands there waiting for us to ask who the fuck that is but neither Sasha or I are going to give her the satisfaction. Besides, Richard has something to share.

'No, no, no,' he is saying. Perhaps. That's the sense of it anyway. He falls to his knees and starts to beg, pawing at the floor where Alice is standing. It's an ugly sight and sound. Sasha is rolling her eyes, seemingly unconvinced by the histrionics on display. I'd say it was coming from the heart myself. It's the sort of craven cowardice I can relate to.

'Stand up!' Alice orders the moaning figure at her feet.

'Help . . . me . . . Help . . . me . . .'

Maybe Richard is actually saying that, maybe it's just my imagination. It gets through to me though. I can't afford a lump in my throat or a very brief moment where my eyes have filled up but one blink later and no one would know. Alice kicks him and he stands up, head bowed, hands covering his eyes. It is now probably crueller to keep him alive than to finish him off cleanly, and also more dangerous unless she is planning to burn out his tongue too. And cut off his fingers in case he wants to type up a statement of confession that will incriminate us all.

There is no getting round it. He will have to go. But there is a lot of Richard and administering the coup de grace is going to be a messy business. Alice must have been thinking something very similar but she has the perfect solution. She selects an industrial-sized frying pan from the rack of cooking implements and uses both hands to bring it down on the top of Richard's head. That gives him pause for thought but he's still standing, or rather staggering around while groaning and gesticulating in the sort of random, hopelessly unskilled manner that would signify heartfelt emotion to the average rock audience. Bryan Ferry himself couldn't have done it any better.

Alice's eyes flash one more time and then she launches another two handed strike with the pan, jumping up to do so. This one catches him on the crown of his head, buckling his legs instantly. He arranges himself in an untidy heap on the floor, or perhaps it's the force of gravity doing that for him – there appears to be no-one home now.

Far from being satisfied with her work Alice starts to put the boot in which looks most unladylike. Sasha and I exchange a glance but it seems prudent to let her get it out of her system. Besides, with any luck she might injure her foot the way she's going at it. She stops eventually, but it turns out she just wants to wipe some spit off her chin.

Soon Alice is swinging the pan again like a woman possessed, not a figure of speech for she is gravely intoning a spell in what might be ancient Norse or Medieval German or something that makes your flesh creep anyway.

Sasha is wincing as each two-handed swipe with the frying pan cleaves into his skull. I never knew she was such a lightweight. It's good to know something can shock her though. With any luck she'll soon be as lily-livered as me and we might get some serious time together on the couch, bathing in the radioactive waves coming off our big television. I like a quiet life, me.

The pan pounds downwards, again and again. Unidentifiable substances are now squirting hither and thither as Alice treats him to the sort of radical body modification that even Sasha wouldn't call art. All things considered I wish she'd stop, as that clanging noise is really getting to me. By now, even Martin Scorsese would feel like stepping in and saying 'Steady on!' but Alice shows no sign of flagging.

We almost miss the knock on the door.

There is instant silence as we contemplate the rest of our lives behind bars. Alice is now a living embodiment of the phrase 'caught red-handed' as the door is pushed slowly open. I wipe the gun on the tail of my shirt then put it on the floor. Then I realise that it might be better to have it in my hand for this might not be the Police. Perhaps the silly eye patch will be enough to frighten whoever this is. Perhaps not. For it is Cathy.

'Richard told me to come over,' she says. She doesn't understand why we look like we have seen a ghost, until she is inside and trying to wipe the blood off her boots. She keeps asking what is going on while we all ignore her.

Alice is mute but triumphant and Sasha is busy watching me chopping out some of Wayne Valentine's white powder onto a dusty mirror. She wants to be first but I fear I am going to have to disappoint her.

'What's that?' says Cathy, almost friendly by her standards. Now I have got something she wants.

'Coke,' I say, 'I think we've all deserved a toot.'

I hand Cathy the mirror and encourage her to do a couple of fat lines. Then Alice graciously condescends to join in. Sasha is glowering now, waiting impatiently for her turn but I shake my head and blow the remaining powder off the mirror right into Cathy's face.

It's gratifying to see a flash of anger in her eyes but it fades before she has wiped the powder off her face. She then licks the residue off her fingers and glares defiantly at me. 'You're about to be out of your body,' I tell her. 'And out of your mind. We could tip you into the Thames and you would drown. You'd enjoy it but you'd still be dead.' For the first time I see fear in her eyes and it's delicious. An image to treasure.

'What is it?' she says.

'Ketamine,' I tell her.

'I could kill you before it comes on,' she says, but her voice lacks her usual certainty. 'Then you won't have anyone to help you while you lose control of your body,' I say.

She takes a moment to adjust to that while Alice starts to tremble violently. She does not appear pleased at the prospect of imminent delirium.

'How long will it last?' asks Alice.

'It'll feel like forever,' I say.

Cathy is pacing about, not so cool, calm and collected now.

'I only came here for the arm,' says Cathy. 'Why don't you just give me the arm?'

'You can make a sculpture out of Richard and Hugh if you like. That should be fun on ketamine.'

'No! You don't understand.'

'Why not? What's the difference?'

'There is no reason to do it! I must have some inspiration from my own life to want to make something into art.'

'So what was the big deal about tattooing Hugh's arm?'

Although I asked the question Cathy starts talking to Sasha.

'He always laughed when I called myself an artist,' says Cathy. 'Sounds crazy I suppose but my father laughed at me too. My brothers did. Even when I got to London I was always told I couldn't be an artist. Using Hugh's body for a canvas seemed very important.'

Sasha nods gravely while I start to tidy up.

'I'm scared,' says Alice.

'Don't worry,' says Sasha, putting an arm around her. 'Ketamine is really beautiful. And euphoric.'

Which is sometimes true, but perhaps not when tripping next to two cadavers – one fresh and one which is more than slightly foxed. I suppose I should leave Cathy alone, now we have won, but I can't resist going for a lap of honour.

'What are you lot going to do now the use of body parts is legitimate? There's nowhere else to go now.'

'You lot?' says Cathy.

'Artists,' I say, trying to make the word sound like 'paedophiles'.

I watch Sasha mulling this over till the solution occurs to me.

'I know,' I say. 'Killing animals.'

'No!' says Sasha, genuinely outraged. 'Anyway, Otto Muehl did it in the sixties.'

'Ronald Mcdonald does it every day. Perhaps he's an artist too.'

Sasha recoils as if I had slapped her in the face with a freshly skinned cat.

For a moment it looks like I might need the gun to protect myself but it is then that Cathy starts to giggle and tell us that she loves us. Soon she is smiling at the wonder of it all. When I feed the arm to the dog Cathy starts laughing, as if she may never stop, while Alice keeps telling us how scared she is.

'Breathe deeply,' says Sasha. 'It's all in the mind.'

We tie them up and while we are cutting some tape for gags Alice says, 'How will we get out of here? When it's over.'

'You'll think of something,' says Sasha, nodding towards the slavering hound. 'Look at you. Three bitches together.'

Once the gags are on Sasha insists on blowing their noses for them, to minimise the chances of death by suffocation. Before we can make our escape there is a brief but intense argument about taking the dog which I resolve by threatening, entirely seriously, to kill myself. Once outside, I wedge the door shut then remember that I forgot to ask Alice who the Dungeonmaster's Apprentice was. I try to kid myself that Sasha will forget about it as we walk off into a cold, grey morning that seems like the last nail in the coffin of autumn.

That night, in Amsterdam, we don't hang weights from our piercings and make slow gentle love while trying to ignore the sound of clanking iron. It's not a case of been there, done that – although we have – it's more that it doesn't seem appropriate while Hugh and Richard are still very much with us. They won't hang around as long as friends and family do, or the first person you kill does, but I'm not entirely convinced that one of Sasha's banishing ceremonies is going to be enough to get rid of them.

We don't play backgammon to determine who will top and who will bottom. Neither do we gently whip each other with the soft leather floggers and then daub minute amounts of diluted propane on each other's skin in the shape of certain occult symbols before setting it briefly alight. Neither do we shave whatever genital stubble has developed during the last few days, nor do we use shaving foam for any other lewd or immoral purpose. We do not pierce any of our soft and tender erogenous zones nor do we widen the existing holes we have already put in. We do not attempt to outdo each other's homemade erotic writing neither do we giggle at the efforts of the professionals.

We do not don gas masks and have vigorous sex until our brains are starved of the requisite amount of oxygen, so generating vivid hallucinations and occasional hints about our past lives. Actually, after what happened to Hugh we may never do this ever again, which is a shame. I used to like that. We leave the restraints, the cock rings, the dildos, the pornos and the red hot pokers in their boxes. The homemade cattle prod lies mute and lonely. Until the next time. We don't have sexual intercourse either.

Even kissing seems a bit sleazy. Holding each other through the hours of darkness seems just about right.